Lightning sent jagged, sizzling streaks against a dark sky. . . .

Minta woke with a start, and gasped. She was drenched to the skin already from the driving rain, and she had to find shelter quickly—the old willow tree was no protection from the storm.

Suddenly she yelped with surprise as strong fingers closed around her wrist. She snapped her head up to meet Chism Talbert's dark, angry eyes.

"You idiot!" he hollered. "You should know better than to stand under a tree during a lightning storm. Come on!"

He nearly lifted her off her feet as he hurried her to the house. The rain beat down on them in a frenzy, and Minta could barely see where she was going. He literally dragged her inside and slammed the door. They stood still for a moment, dripping water onto the wood floor.

A shiver shook Minta's shoulders, and she wrapped her arms around herself. Her T-shirt clung to her like a second skin, and water streamed from her hair down her body.

Chism followed the water's path with his eyes, and despite his cold, soaking clothes, heat exploded within him. Minta looked sensational, he thought. She was drenched, but the way her clothing clung to her body turned him inside out. The young girl he'd never stopped loving had turned into a beautiful woman—and he had to have her. . . .

WHAT ARE *LOVESWEPT* ROMANCES?

They are stories of true romance and touching emotion. We believe those two very important ingredients are constants in our highly sensual and very believable stories in the *LOVESWEPT* line. Our goal is to give you, the reader, stories of consistently high quality that may sometimes make you laugh, sometimes make you cry, but are always fresh and creative and contain many delightful surprises within their pages.

Most romance fans read an enormous number of books. Those they truly love, they keep. Others may be traded with friends and soon forgotten. We hope that each *LOVESWEPT* romance will be a treasure—a "keeper." We will always try to publish

LOVE STORIES YOU'LL NEVER FORGET
BY AUTHORS YOU'LL ALWAYS REMEMBER

The Editors

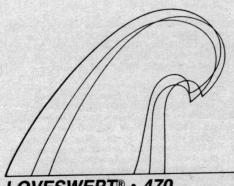

LOVESWEPT® • 470

Joan Elliott Pickart
Memories

BANTAM BOOKS
NEW YORK · TORONTO · LONDON · SYDNEY · AUCKLAND

MEMORIES

A Bantam Book / May 1991

If you would be interested in receiving protective vinyl covers for your Loveswept books, please write to this address for information:

Loveswept
Bantam Books
P.O. Box 985
Hicksville, NY 11802

ISBN 0-553-44116-7

Published simultaneously in the United States and Canada

Bantam Books are published by Bantam Books, a division of Bantam Doubleday Dell Publishing Group, Inc. Its trademark, consisting of the words "Bantam Books" and the portrayal of a rooster, is Registered in U.S. Patent and Trademark Office and in other countries. Marca Registrada. Bantam Books, 666 Fifth Avenue, New York, New York 10103.

*With special thanks
to my Mainers,
Grandma Cushman and Dana*

Memories

Willow Hill
September 5, 1892

Dear Diary,
  Memories.
  The summer is officially over with the setting of the sun on this Labor Day. It is up to me to choose what I shall keep as precious memories of this long, seemingly endless season, and what I shall discard forever as being unimportant.
  I fear I shall discard nearly everything, for it was all so terribly dull, so boring—croquet on the lawn, strolls along the inlet, Sunday afternoon rides in carriages driven by silly young men with their starched white collars and mindless chattering, tea served with cucumber sandwiches and small cakes dribbled with too-sweet frosting.

1

Memories.

What shall I keep from this dreary summer?

We're to stay on here past today instead of proceeding, along with all the other "summer people"—as the natives of Haven Port, Maine, call us—with our usual exodus back to the city. Our house in New York is being totally redecorated, and the workers were not able to finish by today, much to Papa's irritation. I am pleased, though, for I am beginning to prefer the peace and solitude of the Maine coast to the noise and the continual social calls. Fine thoughts for a twenty-year-old spinster. If Mama read this, she'd truly fear that I'll die unwed.

Yet as I sit here in my private, favorite place, the bay window in my bedroom, with darkness dropping like a heavy curtain, I know that the only memories I shall cherish of this summer are of him.

I don't know his name, nor the sound of his voice, nor the color of his eyes. He has hair like sun-kissed wheat, shoulders so wide, and he's tall and strong.

I've watched him from afar, our gardener, the keeper of nature's gifts. Strange yearnings fill me at the merest glimpse of him, even the thought of him. He seems handsome, yet somehow forbidding, and I've never found the courage to venture close enough to speak to him.

It is time to sleep and perhaps . . . perhaps . . . I shall dream of him.

Good night.

Sincerely,

Arminta Masterson

One

Willow Hill
September 4, 1990

Memories.

The word echoed in Minta Westerly's mind, then was quickly followed by shifting scenes from the past, some crystal-clear, others discernible but slightly hazy.

She turned off the ignition of her dark blue BMW, but made no move to get out of the car. Gripping the steering wheel, she stared at the large, three-story house, her gaze lingering on the widow's walk on the second floor.

On the other side of the house was the room that had been hers during the summer so many years ago. She'd adored that bedroom, especially the bay window with cushioned seats, where she'd spent hours daydreaming about the future.

She had been eighteen years old the last time she'd been to Willow Hill in Haven Port, Maine. A lifetime ago, it seemed. She had recently celebrated her thirtieth birthday. Thirty. Lord, where had the years gone?

The house looked the same, she noted, with its multitude of windows that reminded her of knowing eyes that had missed no details of what had taken place there during the past generations. Decades earlier the cedar shingles had been touched by the elements' insistent hand and changed to a lovely, pearly blue-gray color, adding a seasoned charm to the majestic structure.

The sweeping veranda that encircled the house was empty, but as the memories continued to pour over Minta like a waterfall, she saw the white wicker furniture with its marshmallow-soft cushions, heard the sound of voices and laughter, and could almost taste the tart, freshly squeezed lemonade.

Her eighteenth summer. So long ago but, heaven help her, never forgotten. It had been a summer of lazy days, sultry nights, and reckless disregard for society's rules and mores.

It had been a summer of secrets.

It had been the summer of Chism Talbert.

Minta shook her head as though to shake off lingering ghosts that clung like the silken threads of a spider web. Pulling the key from the ignition, she sorted through the jumble on the gold ring until she found the key she knew would unlock the front door to the house. After gathering her purse and sweater from the seat, she opened the car door and stepped out.

Memories.

She shut her eyes for a moment and drew a deep breath, savoring the tangy, fresh scent of the saltwater inlet that lay just beyond the house, down the glorious slope of lush grass that invited a girl to discard her shoes and wiggle her toes in its velvety softness.

She opened her eyes slowly, her gaze sweeping over all within her view—the light fog rolling in off the ocean, the pussy-willow gray of the late-afternoon sky, another house to the left in the far distance.

Minta shivered as a sudden wind brought the hint of a chilly night that would call for a fire in the hearth, a mug of warm milk, then blessed sleep snuggled beneath a comforting handmade quilt.

She turned toward the trunk of the car to get her luggage, then stopped. She had a sudden urge to enter the house, *right now*, as if it were calling to her to hurry.

She hurried up the porch steps and inserted the key in the front door lock, hearing the tumblers easily give way. Her breath caught, and she smiled as she stepped into the living room.

The past twelve years melted away. She was at Willow Hill, and nothing had changed. The hardwood floors gleamed beneath the braided rugs, the oak furniture shone, and she caught a whiff of lemon oil.

The comfortable sofa and chairs were set where they'd always been, inviting her to curl up in their downy depths. The bright splash of color from the floral upholstery was faded now, but still had the magic aura of a field of wildflowers on a sunny day. The flagstone fireplace, topped by a solid oak mantel, held the promise of a crackling fire, with warming orange flames leaping upward.

Minta walked forward, sliding her hand over the smooth, polished wooden ball on the end of the staircase banister. Dropping her belongings onto a chair, she went on, drinking in all she saw: the seascape oil paintings on the walls, the multitude of books on the shelves flanking the fireplace, the framed photographs on the mantel.

She missed no detail, remembering . . . remembering . . . On through the dining room she walked, then hesitated in front of the swinging kitchen door. She imagined she could smell the aroma of apple pie fresh from the oven. Cinnamon and sunshine, laughter and light hearts, youth and its innocence, were all beyond the door to that big, bright yellow room where she'd spent so many wonderful hours.

But, no, she told herself, she wasn't eighteen years old anymore. She was alone at Willow Hill for the first time in her life. There was no cinnamon and sunshine, no laughter filling the rooms of the sturdy old home.

There were only the gray shadows of the darkening sky, and memories.

Her smile faded, and a wave of weariness swept over her as she pushed open the kitchen door and walked into the large room.

At that exact moment the rear door to the house opened and a man entered, one arm curled around a stack of split wood.

Minta gasped. The man halted dead in his tracks. Their eyes met. Time stopped.

A strange buzzing noise roared in Minta's ears, then ceased when she blinked and drew in a much-needed breath of air.

This couldn't be happening, she thought frantically. He was *not* standing there, pinning her in place with his incredible dark eyes. He was not there, his magnificent body clad in jeans and a faded blue flannel shirt, a mature man with a broad chest and wide shoulders, his hair still thick and shiny, still the shade of rich ebony.

He was *not there*.

But he was. Chism Talbert.

She couldn't move. She could only stare . . . and remember.

Dammit to hell, Chism thought, as a cold knot of pain tightened in his gut. *Minta*. She was the last one of the mighty Westerly clan that he'd expected to show up there.

But this was not Minta, the eighteen-year-old girl, he reminded himself. Standing before him was a woman, an incredibly beautiful woman. Gone was the saucy ponytail he remembered, replaced by wavy, shoulder-length auburn hair. She'd grown no taller, still about five-feet-six, and her eyes were the same luscious color of chocolate.

A body that had been skinny was now fashionably slender, with full breasts pushing against a pale green silk blouse, and gently curved hips and long legs encased in khaki slacks.

Heat coiled low in Chism's body, and he knew it for what it was—desire. It fueled the anger brewing within him, and he clenched his jaw hard.

"Hello, Minta," he said, his voice low and rough.

"Hello, Chism," she said, her own voice barely more than a whisper.

Memories, Chism thought when she spoke. She was evoking so many damn memories.

Her soft voice seemed to have created a sensual cloud that hovered in the air. She had a woman's voice now, and its musical sound floated over him, teasing like enticing fingers, fanning the fiery passion deep within him. As well as the anger.

He tore his gaze from her and looked down at the wood he carried.

"I'll get a fire set and ready," he said. "You can light it whenever you want to. This is white birch for a quick start, and I've brought in some oak that will burn longer." For God's sake, Talbert, he told himself, shut up. He was giving a dissertation on firewood as though it were the most important thing he'd ever said. "I'll be out of your way in a few minutes."

As he started across the room, Minta moved quickly from his path, gripping the back of a chair to add support to her trembling legs.

"I—I didn't realize you lived in Haven Port again," she said.

He stopped directly opposite her, and their eyes met once more.

"I don't," he said.

"Oh. You're visiting your father? I mean, he's the one who always tended to opening and closing the homes and—"

"My father is dead," Chism said, then strode out of the room.

"I'm sorry. I didn't know that he . . ." Realizing she was speaking to an empty room, Minta sank onto the chair and pressed her hands to her cold cheeks.

Chism Talbert. She'd assumed when her mother had called the town's general store and left a message that Willow Hill needed to be opened up that Ernest Talbert, Tal, as everyone called him—would do so, as he always had.

Tal was dead? When had he died? He hadn't been that old. Had he been ill? Why had Chism seen to the opening of Willow Hill if he didn't even live in Haven Port? He'd had a cleaning woman in, that was obvious, and Chism himself was seeing to the firewood. Oh, Lord above, Chism was here.

Minta shook her head and stood up. She could handle this, she told herself. He'd get the fire match-ready, then leave. He'd be out of sight, out of mind. No problem.

Oh, who was she kidding? Chism had crept into her thoughts with disturbing regularity since that summer so long ago. Dammit, she didn't want that man in her house. He was dangerous. She'd felt desire begin to pulse within her when he'd looked at her with those mesmerizing dark eyes of his. She'd lost track of time, and place, and . . .

Hello, Minta.

His voice, that rumbling, low, sensuous voice. There was no one who could say her name the way Chism did, making it sound like an intimate caress.

Enough, Arminta Masterson Westerly, she lectured herself. That was absolutely, positively enough. She was going to march across the living room, go to her car, and bring in her luggage.

Chism could putter around with his twigs

and logs to his heart's content, then haul his beautiful carcass out of there and leave her alone. And that, thank you very much, would be that.

Minta lifted her chin and left the kitchen. She strode through the dining room and on into the living room, firmly telling herself that she wouldn't look, not even for a second, toward the fireplace.

Halfway across the living room, she slid a glance toward the fireplace. Her step faltered, then she narrowed her eyes, grabbed her keys off the chair, and stomped out of the house.

How dare that Chism Talbert? she fumed as she unlocked the BMW's trunk. How dare he have changed from a tall, good-looking, lanky nineteen-year-old boy into a beautifully muscular, devastatingly handsome thirty-one-year-old man?

Just who in the blue blazes did he think he was, waltzing into her house after all these years without so much as a by-your-leave? He'd opened the door and walked right back into her . . .

Life?

No! she thought, pulling out her two large suitcases and setting them on the ground. She slammed the trunk closed, then lifted the luggage. Her arms immediately protested the heavy weight. Chism was from a summer long past, she reminded herself, and he should have been forgotten years ago. That the memories of that time still hurt, still plagued her, was something that he would never know.

She was almost to the front door when it was flung open and Chism emerged, a stormy expression on his face. Without a word he took the suitcases from her and turned back into the house.

"You always did take on more than you could handle," he said gruffly.

Minta strode into the house right after him. "And just what is that cryptic statement supposed to mean?"

"Think about it," he said. "Are you using the same bedroom you always did?"

"Yes, but—"

"Fine."

He went up the stairs, carrying the suitcases as easily as if they were filled with feathers. Minta hurried after him. He walked into the second bedroom and set the luggage on the floor.

Minta stepped into the room, a soft "Oh" escaping from her lips. She reverently touched the four-poster bed, the low dresser with a tall mirror attached and a stool in front of it. A small bookcase still held stuffed toys, books, a crystal box of ribbons, an empty soda bottle, a brass candle holder with rivers of hardened pink wax, and countless other pieces of memorabilia.

Each one represented a memory.

Her gaze went to the bay window with the

padded cushions. Through the sparkling-clean glass she could see the inlet below, despite the gathering darkness and fog.

And she saw herself running barefoot through the grass to the water's edge, her face glowing with happiness, her heart singing with joy. She saw herself at eighteen, running into the strong waiting arms of Chism Talbert.

"Memories," she said, not realizing she'd spoken aloud.

Chism's glance slid from Minta to the candle holder, and he vividly remembered how he'd stood by the inlet and eagerly watched for Minta's signal that she was coming to him— the candlelight flickering from the bay window in her bedroom.

His heart would pound and his body would tighten as he counted the agonizing seconds that stretched into minutes. But then Minta was there, in his arms, smelling like flowers, feeling like heaven itself nestled against him, tasting like sweet nectar when he captured her mouth and kissed her, drinking in the very essence of her like a thirsty man.

It had been his nineteenth summer. And when it was over, and the pain of betrayal had darkened his heart and shattered his soul, he'd held true to his vow to never again allow himself to be played for a fool.

"Memories?" he said harshly. "They're a waste of time. Why clutter your brain with old news?" He paused. "I'll be taking off now, unless there's something else you need me to do . . . ma'am. As the hired help, I aim to please."

She whirled to face him, a frown clouding her features.

"Why the sarcasm, Chism?" she asked, a hint of anger in her voice. "If it has anything to do with that last summer I was here, then *you're* the one dealing with old news. Besides, you weren't exactly, shall we say, the injured party."

An expression of surprise showed on Chism's face, then he laughed, a quick, sharp, humorless sound. He folded his arms loosely over his chest and looked at her, no trace of a smile on his lips.

"*I* wasn't the injured party of that fiasco?" He shook his head. "My, my, Arminta, you certainly have changed the facts around to suit your fancy, haven't you? But then, you summer people are used to having things your way, right? We Mainers are simple folk, who face the truth, deal with it, and move on with our lives. *I* wasn't the injured party. That's really something."

She planted her hands on her hips and attempted to stare him down. "It would appear, Mr. Talbert, that *you* are the one whose memory is faulty. However, I hardly think this topic is worth discussing." She paused, and her frown deepened. "No, dammit, we *should* discuss it. Personally, I haven't given that summer a moment's thought since then." Oh, good grief, she thought, what a lie. That summer had haunted her. No, she hadn't given it a moment's thought. She'd given it a thousand, ten thousand, moments of thought. "But you," she went on, "are carrying a grudge. You've also twisted the facts to serve your purpose."

"The hell I have!"

A familiar weariness swept over her, and she wrapped her arms around herself as though warding off a chill. "Oh, Chism, stop it. I don't want to argue with you. I just don't have the energy. Dragging up the events of that summer won't accomplish anything. That's not why I came here."

"Why *did* you come?" he asked, his voice softening as he studied her face. "You're too late to mingle with all the other summer people. Labor Day was yesterday, and they've all left now. What are you doing here?"

"Nothing. I'm on vacation. I'm going to do absolutely nothing."

She *did* look tired, Chism thought. Now that he really paid attention, he could see her exhaustion. It was in her eyes, showed in the purple smudges beneath them, and now that she was giving in to it, it seemed to emanate from her in waves. And there he stood, Mr. Sarcasm, giving her a rough time. Nice guy, Talbert.

But, dammit, how dumb did she think he was? She was actually saying that *he* hadn't been the one to have his heart sliced in two. Oh, yes, they were going to discuss that choice piece of old news. But not now. Not when Minta looked so worn out, so vulnerable, so . . . so damn beautiful.

"I can't picture you doing nothing, Minta," he said. A small smile crept onto his face, then widened. "Arminta Masterson Westerly sitting still, not bouncing around with endless energy? Nope, I just can't see it."

She laughed. "I know. I'm dreading every minute of this." His smile, she thought. Oh, dear heaven, that smile. It lit up his face, softening his obsidian eyes and touching a place within her that was deep, and warm, and secret. "But the doctor said . . . Oh, never mind."

"Are you ill?"

"Oh, no. I'm fashionably stressed-out, as any upwardly mobile career fanatic should be at some time in her fast-lane life. I have a rather high-pressured job with a big ad agency in Manhattan. I haven't had a day off in years, and my body, so says my expensive doctor, is screaming for mercy. So, here I am for a month, prepared to do nothing. Maybe I'll take up needlepoint and make samplers, like some of the earlier Armintas did."

Chism chuckled and shook his head. A shiver coursed through Minta at that dis-

tinctly masculine—and painfully familiar—
sound. Their eyes met, and their smiles slowly
faded.

As they stared at each other, a strange
sensuality seemed to weave around them,
pulling at them with threads unseen but felt.
Hearts raced and desire pulsed in a body soft
and curved, and in a body rugged and hard.
Memories of days and nights long past inter-
twined with a new, burning passion.

They moved at the same time, closing the
distance between them, forgetting the pain of
the past, erasing the years.

Chism wrapped his arms around Minta,
and her hands floated upward to encircle his
neck. Then slowly, very slowly, he lowered his
head, and his mouth melted over hers.

The kiss was all, and more, that they both
remembered their kisses had been. They were
a woman and a man now, now a girl and a boy.
And as they filled their senses with new and
remembered sensations, they created more
memories.

Minta's breasts were heavy, yearning for the
soothing lave of Chism's tongue, the caress of
his strong but gentle hands. Desire pulsed
insistently within her, demanding satisfaction. Too dazed by the sudden splendor to be
shocked, she realized she wanted to make love
with Chism, to be one with him . . . again.

Minta! Chism thought as he gathered her
closer. His Minta. He wanted her, ached for

her. And he would have her, because she was his. She had always been his. They would make love, beautiful love, then lie close, whispering in the dark until it was time for her to hurry back to Willow Hill. . . .

No, he thought foggily. That was then, during that last summer. The summer of her betrayal. This was now. What in the hell was he doing?

He stiffened and broke the kiss. Dragging Minta's arms from his neck, he took a step backward, his breathing rough. She opened her eyes, and he saw they were clouded with confusion and desire.

"That was a mistake," he said, his voice raw with passion. "It shouldn't have happened."

Minta blinked as though awakening from a deep sleep. "I . . ." She shook her head. "Yes, you're right. It was a mistake. We're strangers really, after all these years. We don't know each other, who we've become. You could be married and have six children."

"I've never married," he said quietly.

"No? I haven't, either. I've been concentrating on my career and . . ." She drew a shuddering breath. "I think it would be best if we forgot what just happened, Chism. It was wrong, it was—"

"Fine," he interrupted. "Enjoy your vacation." He turned and strode toward the door. "You'll get the hang of doing nothing."

"Chism?"

He stopped and looked at her over his shoulder.

"I'm sorry about your father. I liked him very much, and he was always kind to me. He told such wonderful stories about his days on the whaling boats. I just wanted you to know that I'm sorry he's gone."

Chism stared at her for a long moment, then nodded once and left the room.

Minta didn't move. She pressed trembling fingers to her kiss-swollen lips and simply stood there, blanking her mind, thinking of nothing, as the darkness of night closed in around her.

Willow Hill
September 7, 1892

Dear Diary,
    Blue. His eyes are blue, like a summer sky.
    Or bluebonnet flowers, or a crystal clear pond of water, or the sapphires in the necklace Mama and Papa gave me on my sixteenth birthday.
    But I shouldn't compare the blue of his eyes to anything that already exists in this world, for he is too rare, too special, to be placed among that which is ordinary.
    Oh, I was so bold today. Wearing my new yellow gingham day-dress and carrying the matching parasol, I strolled leisurely through the garden where he was working.
    My heart was pounding so wildly, I feared he would surely hear. My cheeks were flushed, and I hoped he would—if he noticed—attribute

21

it to the unusually hot weather. My knees were trembling so violently, I imagined I would swoon at his feet if he spoke to me.

But he didn't speak. As I passed him, humming softly, as if I hadn't a care in the world, he turned his head and our gazes met. Was it for seconds? Minutes? Hours? How is one to know when it seems time has stopped?

As I sit here in my bay window, reliving that wonderful moment, I cannot remember if I smiled at him. How distressing to wonder what expression he saw on my face.

Even more disturbing is what I glimpsed in his beautiful blue eyes. Anger.

What has caused his fury? How I yearn to know, and to soothe his inner turmoil.

I ache to hear his voice speaking my name, and to know his name, and how it shall sound as it whispers from my lips.

Such brash, bold thoughts. Such strange, fluttering sensations swirl within me as I sit here alone thinking of him. He is so beautiful, my angry blue-eyed gardener.

I know I shall not be content until I have heard his voice. I risk the wrath of Mama and Papa should they catch me speaking with him, but I must do it. I must.

'Tis time to sleep now, dear diary, and I shall dream of the blue of his eyes.

Good night.

Sincerely,

Arminta Masterson

Two

Willow Hill
September 5, 1990

Blue.

Minta stood at the bay window and gazed at the sky, a smile on her face. She'd forgotten how glorious a morning in Maine could be. She'd slept soundly for the first time in weeks, awakening to a room filled with sunshine.

She'd showered, dressed in jeans and a T-shirt as blue as the sky, and now was ready for breakfast. She was actually hungry, she thought as she left the bedroom. She'd eaten by rote the past months, having no appetite to speak of. At times she'd resorted to writing a memo to herself, reminding herself to eat lunch at some point in her hectic day.

Hectic day, she mentally repeated as she

entered the bright, cheerful kitchen. Well, she'd certainly come full circle, because she had absolutely no idea how to fill the days that stretched before her like a blank blackboard.

Her buoyant mood slowly dissipated, and she was frowning by the time she sat down at the table with a mug of coffee, and a plate of scrambled eggs, bacon, and two pieces of toast.

What did Chism do with himself all day? she wondered. Even more, what was he doing in Haven Port since he'd made it clear he didn't live there? Why had he tended to opening Willow Hill for her?

And why had she dreamed about him last night? The dreams had been filled with sensual scenes of the two of them, kissing and caressing and—

"Stop it, Arminta," she muttered, then shoveled in a forkful of eggs.

The previous evening she'd actually convinced herself that she'd dismissed from her mind the kiss she'd shared with Chism. But her dreams had proven how deeply that kiss had affected her, and she'd awakened once in the night with his name on her lips and desire running rampant through her trembling body.

Ridiculous, she told herself, lifting her coffee mug. Such adolescent behavior for a mature, sophisticated woman. In the light of the new day she understood what had happened. Due to her fatigue and the nostalgic return to

Willow Hill, her emotions had been hurled back in time to that fateful summer of long ago. She'd been exhausted, thus vulnerable. When Chism appeared . . . Well, it all made sense now. End of story.

Satisfied with her rationalization, she took a sip of coffee, then nearly dropped the mug into her eggs when a knock sounded at the back door. She set the mug firmly on the table and crossed the room to open the door.

It was Chism.

Her heart skipped a beat and her breath caught as she stared at him, missing no detail of his magnificent body clad in worn jeans and a faded black T-shirt.

"Good morning," she managed to say. So much for her brilliant theory regarding her reactions to this man, she thought. He aroused her slumbering sensuality simply by standing there, meeting her gaze with those damnable dark eyes of his. If she gave him one hint of the effect he had on her, she'd wring her own neck. "What can I do for you this lovely morning, Mr. Talbert?"

She could knock off looking so beautiful, Chism thought sullenly. She could stay out of his dreams, like the ones that had tormented his aching body through the long night. She could be someone else, anyone else, except herself, except Minta.

"The—" he started, then cleared his throat when he heard the gritty tone of his voice.

"The dock is in bad shape. It'll never hold up under the winter storms if it isn't repaired. Do you want me to go ahead and fix it? I'll have to get some new lumber for parts of it."

Minta frowned. "Chism, why don't you come in? I'm rather confused about why you're tending to these chores if you don't live here." She moved back to allow him to enter. "Would you like some coffee?"

"Okay. One cup, then if you do want the dock repaired, I'd better get to it. There's a storm due in by late afternoon."

He stepped into the room, and as she closed the door behind him, he glanced at the table. "Your eggs are getting cold," he said. "I'll pour my coffee. Where are the mugs?"

Minta pointed to the cupboard next to the sink, then sat back down at the table. She stole glances at Chism as he moved around the kitchen, preparing his coffee.

Masculine magnetism, she decided. That was a good description of what he possessed. An intangible something emanated from him, shouting "male" in capital letters. He didn't flaunt it, like some of the men at her health club did. Chism was simply being Chism.

Had he been *this* compelling at nineteen, she wondered, as a youth just beginning to fill out, beginning to become a man? She'd been drawn to him even back then, as though by some invisible force.

Oh, how deeply she had loved him. She'd

given him herself, her innocence, then had wept tears of joy, not of regret. He had been the center of her existence, her raison d'être. She'd placed her heart and soul in his hands—and he'd crushed them into a million pieces.

She shook her head to dispel the shadowy ghosts from the past, then took a bite of her toast. A dollop of the sweet butter clung to her upper lip, and she fumbled on her lap for her napkin.

As Chism approached the table, he stopped, his gaze riveted on Minta. As she shook out her napkin, the tip of her tongue skimmed over her lips, catching the errant dab of butter.

That simple gesture gave fire to the familiar and yet unwelcome heat that had been surging through his body since the day before. In his mind he saw *his* tongue tracing the outline of her lips, licking away the creamy butter, then delving into the sweet darkness of her mouth to dance and duel with her own tongue.

His anger flared once again along with his ardor, and he frowned as he strode to the table. He flipped a chair around and straddled it, resting his forearms on the top and wrapping his hands around the mug of steaming coffee.

Nice try, Talbert, he thought dryly. For a fleeting moment he'd had the irrational idea that the chair would act as a protective barrier between himself and Minta. A chair wouldn't do it, any more than the years and distance had.

"Chism?" she said, bringing him from his reverie. "If this is none of my business, just say so. But why are you doing the type of work your father always did if you don't even live here?"

He took a deep swallow of coffee, then met her gaze. "It's none of your business."

Minta got to her feet to carry her empty plate to the sink. "That's certainly clear enough," she said, setting the plate down. "I'm sure my family would appreciate your fixing the dock. You can submit the bill to me and I'll write you a check."

Chism drained his mug and stood, then a moment later thudded the mug onto the counter next to her plate. "Fine."

Too close, he thought. He was standing too close to her. He could smell the light floral perfume that she'd always worn, as well as the fresh aroma of soap and shampoo. Her hair was shiny, beckoning to him to sink his fingers into it and watch the silky strands slide through his fingers. Dammit, he had to get out of that house and away from Minta Westerly.

"I'll go for the supplies," he said, "then start on the dock. See ya."

He turned and strode out of the kitchen, closing the door behind him with a quiet click. Minta stood perfectly still, listening to the silence that settled heavily over the room. The echo of Chism's deep voice grew fainter, then was gone. All was quiet. It was as though, she thought, Chism had taken the vitality, the sparkle, of the day with him, leaving everything dull and drab and silent.

Minta shook herself. That was ridiculous. It was still a glorious clear-sky day in Maine. She was going to put Chism Talbert firmly from her mind and enjoy her vacation. She'd . . .

"Do what all day?" she said aloud, throwing up her hands. "Arminta, shape up."

Half an hour later Minta planted her hands on her hips and nodded in approval. She'd rescued her old purple bicycle from the carriage house and propped it against a tree. She'd sprayed it with the hose to wash away the dust and cobwebs, which also resulted in a multitude of purple paint flakes littering the grass. The bike was a rusty, dented mess, but the tires seemed to be holding since she'd pumped them up, and now the water had dried.

"Fantastic," she said, smiling happily.

So many memories were connected with the dilapidated bike. It had been canary yellow the year she'd been nine and discovered it waiting for her at Willow Hill. Her parents had sent it on ahead before leaving New York for the summer in Maine.

During her thirteenth summer, she remembered as she walked the bicycle from the rear of the house toward the road, she'd painted her trusty bike purple. Passionate Purple, a color befitting a girl who had grown up, who had become an official teenager.

It had been a very purple summer. Her bathing suit, the majority of her shorts and tops, and even her sneakers had all been purple. It was her "statement of adulthood," she'd solemnly told her questioning mother. But said mother had drawn the line at dark purple lipstick.

Minta laughed softly. So many lovely, silly, and sentimental memories she had tucked away, she realized. Happiness had come so easily in those days of youth and innocence.

And now? she asked herself as she reached the road. Was she happy? Such a simple question, yet the answer was surprisingly elusive. It was also a question she hadn't asked herself in more years than she could remember. She'd simply lived her pressure-filled, fast-paced life without stopping to rest, or to take an emotional inventory.

She got on the bicycle, gasped as she wobbled and weaved for the first hundred feet or so, then smiled in satisfaction when she got the hang of the rhythm. The old saying was true: Once you learned to ride a bicycle, you never really forgot how.

One of her girlfriends, she recalled, had said that about making love. "Sex?" she'd said. "Well, hell, Minta, it's like riding a bike. Experience it, and you're set for life. You'll always know how to do it."

But there was a tremendous difference between having sex and making love, Minta had argued. Her friend had labeled her a romantic, and the conversation had shifted to another topic.

Minta picked up speed, enjoying the feel of the wind against her face, inhaling all the aromas it carried. Everything was so fresh and clean, she thought. And incredibly quiet. It seemed a world away from the hustle, bustle, and noise of Manhattan. Oh, what an absolutely glorious day.

Sex and making love, she mused as she peddled steadily on. Yes, there *was* a tremendous difference between the two. She'd had a few serious-at-the-time relationships over the past years, but there'd always been something missing, a void, and she'd realized that what she shared with that man just wasn't enough to sustain a lifelong commitment. She hadn't been *in* love, so their intimacy had been nudged into the having-sex category, rather than into the one labeled making love.

No, she hadn't been in love, truly in love, with all its wondrous magic, since . . .

"Chism," she whispered. "Oh, damn."

She increased her speed, as though she could outdistance her own thoughts, leaving the memories of the past behind as she sped down the road.

With a sense of relief, she saw the town of Haven Port coming into view. There would be people to talk to and things to see there, and she could escape her disturbing thoughts. She could put Chism Talbert back on a dusty shelf in her brain, where he belonged.

Little had changed in Haven Port, Maine, she realized as she stopped the bike in front of the general store. One or two of the buildings housed something different from before. A craft store filled one, and she spotted a new gift shop with wind chimes, most in the form of sea gulls, hanging in the window.

The gas station was still on the far corner, then the laundromat, the post office, the café, and a few other establishments designed to entice the tourists.

Minta leaned the bike against the side of the steps leading up to the old general store. As she opened the door, tiny copper bells tingled, announcing her arrival.

Memories.

She closed the door and stood perfectly still, drinking in the familiar scents and sights. So many memories of ice-cream cones and peppermint sticks, of freshly baked bread that she'd wrap in a red-and-white checked tea towel and nestled in the basket on her bike. She'd zoom back down the road to Willow Hill, where her parents were waiting to enjoy the crusty loaf.

And over there . . . yes, the magazine rack, where she'd stand with her friends, who also came for the summer, and sigh at the pictures of the handsome movie stars on the covers.

Then that last summer, she'd stood in that very store and shared an orange soda with Chism. The empty bottle still sat on the shelf in her bedroom.

"Well, land's sake," a woman exclaimed, jolting Minta from her memories. "Is that you, Minta Westerly? Now haven't you grown up to be one beautiful woman?"

Minta smiled and crossed the room to the counter. A short, round, gray-haired woman leaned over the counter with outstretched arms, and Minta hugged her.

"Hello, Mrs. Cushing," she said, smiling as she straightened. "You look wonderful, exactly the same, and you still smell like vanilla, my favorite perfume."

"Because I still bake every chance I get," Lily Cushing said, laughing. "And I've the pounds to prove it. I'll go to my grave smelling like vanilla. I swear, Minta honey, you swept the years away when you walked in that door. The same thing happened when Chism first came home. He stepped in here and it was suddenly a dozen years ago."

Oh, please, Minta silently begged, don't go on about Chism. Too many memories were assaulting her at every turn as it was.

"That Chism," Lily continued, "turned out to be a fine, good-looking man." She laughed. "There was a spell there when I thought he'd spend his days in jail, the way he carried on. He'd go roaring up and down on that motorcycle he'd built from scrap pieces and . . . Oh, he was a wild, reckless boy, that one. I can remember the time he—"

"Yes, well," Minta interrupted, "I just wanted to say hello. I'll be here for a month."

"Your mama said the house would be open for a month, but she didn't say who was coming. This was the first summer I can ever remember that Willow Hill wasn't used. Then up you pop *after* the summer people."

"My parents have come every year," Minta said, "but my father had business in London this summer, so they decided to make a vacation of it. I think my mother is a bit sorry. Summer to her always meant coming to Willow Hill. She missed it terribly this year."

Lily cocked her head to one side. "What are you doing here after Labor Day?"

"Oh, just taking a break from a very hectic life. One year slipped into the next, and I didn't take a vacation, just pushed on. I'm exhausted. I'm going to lie around and recuperate at Willow Hill."

"And then?"

"Then?" Minta repeated, in confusion.

"Yes, what then, Minta?" Lily asked. "You just going to go back to that rat race in the city for another dozen years before you take time out for Haven Port and Willow Hill again? Your being here alone tells me you're not married. When are you going to settle down, have some babies?"

Lily laughed. "I asked Chism the same thing when he came back. 'Chism Talbert,' I said, 'it's time to get yourself a wife and start a family.' All I got from him was a look that was a storm brewing."

Lily clicked her tongue. "You young people today . . . All you think about is fancy careers so as you can buy fancy cars and fancy houses. Whatever happened to a fire in the hearth and a baby on your knee?"

"Chism has a *fancy* career?" Minta asked. "If that's true, why is he fixing our dock? Why did he tend to opening Willow Hill?"

"Well, you'll have to ask him 'bout that. It's his private business." Lily's eyes widened. "Mercy, where has my old mind gone off to? I remember that last summer you and Chism were here. Why, you two were canoodlin' to beat the band."

"Canoodlin'?" Minta said, feeling a warm flush on her cheeks. "Just what exactly does that mean?"

"It means," a deep voice said, "innocent

goings on between a girl and boy. Very innocent."

Minta spun around to see Chism striding across the room. He'd apparently entered the building through the rear door. He walked slowly toward her, his gaze locked with hers, then halted directly in front of her.

"Mrs. Cushing," he said, still looking at Minta, "Minta and I were *not* canoodlin' that summer. Isn't that right, Minta?"

"I . . . W-well . . ." she stuttered then glared at him.

Damn the man, she thought. He was toying with her, playing word games. No, they hadn't been "canoodlin'," for Pete's sake, because their relationship had been far from innocent. It had been deep and rich, real and earthy. They'd been in love, they'd made love.

"Oh, pshaw," Lily said, laughing merrily. "I know better. Don't figure anyone else knew, but there's not much gets past Lily Cushing. You two were canoodlin', all right, then . . . poof . . . you were both gone, and all those years passed. Well, what goes around, comes around, and here you both are back in Haven Port." She nodded. "Where you belong."

Chism shifted his gaze to Lily, and there was a definite edge to his voice when he spoke. "Belong? Aren't you forgetting something, Mrs. Cushing? Minta isn't a native. She's one of the summer people."

Lily folded her arms over her ample bosom.

"There's summer folks, and then there's summer folks, Chism Talbert. Minta Westerly never put on airs when she was here. You couldn't tell her from the Mainers all those summers. And she's here right now, *after* Labor Day. There, that proves my point. You're both back where you belong, and you won't budge me on my opinion."

Chism started to retort, but laughed instead. Minta felt a shiver course through her at the sound of his deep, full laugh.

"I won't say another word," he said, holding up both hands in a gesture of surrender. "When a New Englander makes up his—in this case, her—mind, there's no talking to them. Might as well discuss it with a tree for all the good it'll do you."

"Ayuh," Lily said, lifting her chin. "And don't you forget it."

"No, ma'am," Chism said, still smiling. "I need some nails. I didn't find what I wanted in my dad's supply to fix the Westerlys' dock."

"That's surprising," Lily said. "Your daddy was a true Mainer. He never threw anything away. If there's no nails to your liking, it's due to his running out, not throwing out. Get what you need, Chism, then write it in the ledger as owing me. Minta, did I send enough food up to Willow Hill for a spell?"

"Oh, my, yes. There's enough for an army."

"Well, eat it. You're as skinny as a white

birch stripped bare of bark. Chism, don't you think she's too skinny?"

"Oh, good Lord," Minta muttered.

Chism shoved his hands into the back pockets of his jeans and began a very slow, very thorough scrutiny of Minta's body. She felt seared by his penetrating gaze, heat swirling within her with alarming intensity as he visually traced every inch of her.

"In my opinion—" he finally began.

"Mr. Talbert," she interrupted. There was a false sweetness to her voice as her eyes sparked with anger. "I would highly recommend, sir, that if you plan to live past your next breath, you give very, *very* careful thought to your opinion before you express it."

Lily cackled with laughter, obviously enjoying the entire scene.

A slow smile crept onto Chism's face. "In my opinion, Miss Westerly, you look fine, just fine. But what you need to reach perfection is . . . a bottle of orange soda."

Willow Hill
September 8, 1892

Dear Diary,
   Rain.
   How could Mother Nature do this to me? It has rained since before dawn, great, heavy sheets of water, as though all the angels in the sky were crying.
   I was held captive in the house the entire day, roaming from room to room, often staring out the windows with the hope of seeing a tiny patch of blue that might grow bigger.
   But it just rained, and rained, and rained.
   So my beautiful blue-eyed gardener never

came to Willow Hill today. Oh, the injustice of it, the unfairness.

Where does he live? What does he do during the long hours of a day such as this? How does he spend his leisure time when he's not tending to the garden?

Mama was aware of my restlessness and urged me to sit with her by the fire and attempt again—although it is an impossible quest—to become adept at needlepoint. I despise the silly projects, though, and grow weary and frustrated at the tangling threads and how my tiny stitches go this way and then that way.

All the while that I pretended to concentrate on the needlepoint, I was aware of a strange force gripping my soul, making me yearn to dash from the house into the storm, and feel the rain on my face, the whipping of the wind against my body.

I want to run free.

I want to run to him.

I should be horrified at this decadent desire, yet the need to speak to him, to hear his voice, perhaps even to see him smile, is so powerful, it overshadows all propriety, all sense of right and wrong.

Tears have filled my eyes as I write. I am uncertain as to what has made me cry, except I know I am empty and cold, and so very lonely.

*I must go to my bed before Mama sees the
glow of my lamp and wonders anew at my
behavior.*

Good night.
Sincerely,
Arminta Masterson

Three

Willow Hill
September 5, 1990

Rain.

It was on its way, Chism thought, as he heard thunder rumbling in the distance.

He drove another nail into the fresh wood of the dock, using—as he had since he'd begun the project—more force than was necessary.

The storm was building, he mused, and just might match the intensity of the one building within *him.* Why had he said it? Why had he made that asinine remark to Minta about having an orange soda?

The moment the words had escaped his lips, hovering like tangible entities in the air, the memory had slammed into his mind of a sultry summer day when he and Minta had stood in that general store and shared an orange soda. Minta had insisted on keeping the bottle, he remembered, and he'd seen it on the bookshelf when he'd carried her luggage to her room.

How could something as ordinary, as idiotic, as a bottle of orange soda cause such inner turmoil? When he'd spoken the words, Minta's eyes had widened in shock, and he'd known that she recalled that day just as vividly as he.

The arrival of Old Man Ryan, shuffling into the store, had rescued them. Minta had mumbled her good-bye to Lily Cushing, then raced out the door. Chism had found the nails he needed, and beat a hasty retreat before Lily could get on her canoodlin' tangent again.

And that was another thing, Talbert, he admonished himself. He'd taunted Minta with his veiled innuendoes about them not being involved in *innocent* canoodlin'.

When the time was right, and when he and Minta were alone, he intended to have some answers to some very old, very painful questions. But he sure as hell had no business saying what he had in front of someone as perceptive and observant as Lily Cushing.

Thunder rumbled again, and Chism glanced up at the sky. Dark, angry clouds were rolling in like giant, rushing waves.

A few more nails, he decided, then he'd better pack it up and head out of there. He assumed that Miss Minta Westerly was safely inside the house, having the good sense to get in before the rain started.

Miss Minta Westerly was *not* inside the house.

After escaping from the store, she'd ridden her bike leisurely along the road out of town, veering onto side paths as the mood struck. She'd returned home at noon, had some lunch, then started out again on her trusty purple machine.

As she'd ridden away from town this time, her glance had fallen on the majestic willow tree on top of a rise at the edge of the Westerly property. That tree had given Willow Hill its name, and Minta had spent hours beneath it, concocting daydreams, as she was sure all the Armintas who preceded her had.

She'd walked the bike up the incline and laid it down, then stretched out on the ground within the shelter of the drooping branches. As she watched the sun dancing through the leaves above her, she felt herself become drowsy, her eyes drifting closed.

The willow tree of Willow Hill, she thought dreamily. One daring night she and Chism had made love beneath that tree, exquisite, beautiful love. The low-hanging branches had created a private chamber, a world away from reality.

Chism, she mused, half-asleep. And orange soda.

Her eyes flew open, then narrowed in anger as she recalled the scene in the store.

Chism Talbert was despicable. His canoodlin' nonsense, then his reference to orange soda, had caused her temper to flare nearly out of control. Thank goodness she'd got out of the store before she'd said anything more. Lily Cushing was sharp as a tack, and wouldn't have missed one detail of the interchange between Minta and Chism. At least Minta hadn't given Lily any further food for thought.

She closed her eyes again.

Chism Talbert, she decided, could take a long walk off that short dock he was in the process of repairing. She was *not* going to ruin this delightful time beneath the wonderful old tree by chasing thoughts of him around in her brain. Her mind was now blank, empty.

And she was . . . so very . . . deliciously sleepy.

The storm that had been announcing its arrival for nearly an hour seemed determined to make an impressive entrance. Instead of sprinkling a final warning with raindrops, the clouds opened and dumped their heavy cargo.

Pounding rain fell, as well as 20 degrees of the temperature. Thunder roared, rather than repeating its previous subdued rumble, and lightning sent jagged, sizzling streaks across the dark sky.

As the cold rain assaulted Minta, she sat bolt upright with a gasp, fully awake.

"Oh, Lord," she exclaimed, jumping to her feet.

She was already drenched to the skin and shivering, the heavy branches of the willow tree a useless umbrella against the chilling rain. She pushed her streaming hair out of her eyes and grabbed the handlebars of the bike. When the bike lurched forward, she looked down and groaned with dismay. The front tire was flat.

The next instant she yelped with surprise as a large hand yanked the bike away, then strong fingers closed around one of her wrists. She snapped her head up to meet Chism Talbert's dark, angry eyes.

"You idiot!" he hollered above the noise of the storm. "You should know better than to stand under a tree in a lightning storm. Come on."

He nearly lifted her off her feet as he strode out from beneath the tree.

"Hey," said Minta, attempting in vain to free her wrist from his iron grip. "What about my bike?"

"The hell with your bike. With any luck that stupid purple paint will wash off. I liked it better when it was yellow. Now shut up and let's go."

"But— Oh!"

Chism started running, and Minta felt as though she were nearly airborne as she raced down the incline with him, her wrist still held firmly in his grasp. The rain beat down on them with a vengeance as it was whipped into a frenzy by the roaring wind. Minta could barely see as they ran on.

They finally reached the house, and Chism flung open the kitchen door that Minta hadn't bothered to lock. He literally dragged her into the room, then slammed the door shut behind him.

The pair stood still for a moment, gulping in air as puddles formed at their feet from the water dripping off them.

A shiver shook Minta's shoulders and she wrapped her arms around herself. Her T-shirt was clinging to her like a second skin, her breasts clearly defined. Water streamed from her hair, sliding over her taut nipples like a charted river.

Chism's gaze followed the water's path, and despite his cold, soaked clothes, heat exploded within him.

Minta looked sensational, he thought. She was drenched, but the way her T-shirt was plastered to her was turning him inside out. Her hair was a wet, wild mess, and made her appear reckless and vitally alive. Lord, Minta Westerly was a beautiful woman.

"Oh, I'm so cold," she said, her teeth beginning to chatter. She hurried into the bathroom off the kitchen and returned with two fluffy towels. "Here," she said as she handed one to him. "For all the good it will do."

He dragged the towel down his face. "What in the hell did you think you were doing, standing under a tree like that in a lightning storm? That wasn't exactly genius-level behavior."

Minta squeezed the ends of her hair with the towel. "I wasn't standing there," she said. "I was leaving there. I fell asleep under the tree, and the next thing I knew—swoosh!—a waterfall came pouring over me. How did you know I was up there?"

"I was in my truck ready to take off, and I saw your bike when the wind moved the branches of the tree for a moment. The ground is too soft to drive up there, so I had to run. I figured you were under the tree. See the bike, you see Minta. The dynamic duo, the inseparable pair."

She smiled. "That's a fact. That bike and I have been together for many years and many miles."

"I know. I remember when you got it. I figured you'd kill yourself that first summer by crashing into a tree. I'd never seen such an uncoordinated bike rider in my life." He paused, and his gaze shifted to a spot on the far wall. "It was a great bike, though. Shiny and new, and bright yellow. I can recall having a dream one night that the bike was mine, and I was riding along the road with the wind in my face and—"

He blinked, as though dragging himself back to the present from a memory-filled place. He cleared his throat, then frowned at Minta again.

"You really screwed it up," he said gruffly, "when you painted it purple."

She cocked her head to one side as she looked at him intently. "I didn't even know you then, Chism."

"I was around. A few years later I started working with my father, tending to the needs of the summer people. I knew the exact minute that yellow bike arrived at Willow Hill."

Minta felt the unexpected ache of tears in her throat as she envisioned Chism, the young boy, yearning to have a shiny yellow bike and knowing he never would.

She knew little about his youth. He'd been reluctant to talk about it, even during the lazy, contented times after their lovemaking. His mother had packed up and walked out, he'd told her, when he was five. He and his father were close, devoted to each other.

When Chism had taken her to the small frame house where he and his father lived, she'd viewed it through romantic eyes, seeing it as quaint and cozy. Now she realized that their house and all the others that stood jammed together across the inlet were shabby and run-down.

It was the summer people of Haven Port who had the big, sprawling homes and all the luxuries. It was the summer people's children who received shiny new yellow bikes.

During her eighteenth summer, love had been the equalizer, and rose-colored glasses had kept her from really understanding how Chism had always lived, and what he'd never had.

Minta shivered, not certain if it was from discovering the shallowness of her youthful perceptions, or from the cold.

"This is nuts," Chism said. "We're standing here freezing to death. I'll go light a fire. You go shower and change into dry clothes. I'm staying put for a while until the worst of the storm is over, since I'm not in the mood to get struck by lightning."

"You'll catch pneumonia in those wet things. My father has clothes here, Chism, and I'm sure they'd fit you. Go into the end bedroom upstairs and help yourself. Oh, I'm so cold." She turned and hurried from the room.

Chism watched her go, then glanced out the window at the raging storm.

Damn, he thought, he wanted to get out of there, away from Arminta Masterson Westerly. The sensual power she had over him was dangerous, and it angered him. He'd never expected to see her again, but there she was. And heaven help him, he wanted her, wanted to make love with her and find the ecstasy of release his aching manhood demanded.

Lightning flashed, then thunder boomed in the next instant. With a resigned sigh, Chism left the kitchen and slowly climbed the stairs. He stopped for a moment outside the closed bathroom door, hearing the water running in the shower.

He envisioned Minta naked, the warm water sliding seductively over her dewy skin, caressing her full breasts and gliding down her long, satiny legs. As he felt the stirrings of arousal, he swore under his breath and strode with heavy steps down the long hallway to the master bedroom.

After Minta dressed in a fleecy Kelly-green jogging suit, she sat on the stool in front of her dresser and blow-dried her hair.

This, she thought, was not a good idea. She was alone in the house with Chism Talbert. It was as though they'd been cut off from the world by the storm, and just like that summer long past, no one knew they were together.

So? she asked herself. What was she afraid of? It wasn't as though Chism were a stranger she'd given shelter to from the rain. She'd known him for years, a lifetime, it seemed.

There was nothing to be frightened of, she told herself, Chism wasn't about to attack her, ravish her body while the storm blew out its fury. This wasn't a sinister gothic novel, this was reality.

And the reality was, she admitted with a weary sigh, that she was frightened of *herself*, of her emotional and physical reactions to Chism. She was acutely aware of every marvelous masculine inch of him, as well as being aware, for the first time in a very long while, of her own femininity.

Her senses were strangely heightened, magnifying her awareness of every part of Chism. Sensuality seemed to glow within her, making her body hum and desire pulse.

She wanted him.

There it was in all its lustful glory, she thought dryly. She wanted to make love with Chism Talbert.

Why?

To attempt to recapture her lost youth by making love with her first lover?

No, that wasn't it. She yearned to experience, to cherish, the incredible *magic* that had not been hers since her summer of Chism. Just once more, before she returned to her fast-paced life and became swallowed up in its madness, once more . . . with Chism.

Minta stumbled to her feet, setting the hairbrush and blow dryer down with shaking hands.

This was ridiculous, she admonished herself. The mental road she'd just traveled was absurd. She had no intention of making love with Chism.

She was an adult, a successful career woman, who survived in a cutthroat business. She could handle being alone with Chism until the storm passed—so long as she kept her mind in the present and didn't indulge in the dangerous luxury of memories.

No memories, Minta, she ordered herself as she left the bedroom.

As she stepped into the hallway, she glanced to the left and saw that the door to the master bedroom was open, indicating Chism was no longer in there. Descending the stairs, she realized she'd postponed her reappearance so long, Chism had finished showering and dressing, even though she'd begun before him.

When she reached the first floor, she began walking slowly across the living room, then stopped. Chism had his back to her as he hunkered down in front of the fire. He placed another log on the leaping flames, closed the screen, then stood, staring into the fire.

He was wearing a pair of her father's old jeans that were a tad short, and a flannel shirt that was tight across his broad shoulders, with sleeves that didn't reach his wrists.

She could remember that when she was a

very little girl, she'd thought there was no one as tall and strong as her dad. Childish perceptions again, because Chism was obviously a bigger man than her father.

How many other things had she been wrong about? she wondered. What had she seen but not fully comprehended, heard but not understood?

What strange thoughts, she mused, and they stemmed from being at Willow Hill, being pulled mentally and emotionally between the past and the present. During this storm, though, while Chism was in the house, she was going to remain firmly in the present.

The room was dim because of the heavy rain clouds, the brightest light coming from the fire. It cast a warm glow over Chism as he stood in front of it, and a tingling sensation danced along Minta's spine. She reached out and snapped on the lamp that stood on an end table.

Chism turned slowly to face her. As their eyes met, neither moved, neither spoke.

His muscles rigid with tension, Chism felt as though he were standing too close to a powder keg, waiting for it to explode, wondering what the aftermath would be. Dreading it, yet eagerly awaiting it.

He was not going to ignite the fuse, though. Somehow he had to keep things light and casual between himself and Minta. Which meant that this was definitely *not* the time to demand answers to his questions about that long-ago summer.

"So," he said, his voice too loud in the stillness, "do you think it will stop raining?"

Minta looked surprised, then she smiled.

"Always has," she said, and laughed. "I haven't thought of that silly Downeast joke in years. My favorite, though, is the one your father told me over and over."

"Ah, yes," Chism said, smiling too. "I heard that your horse dropped dead."

"Ayuh," Minta said. "First time I ever seen her do that."

Their laughter seemed to fill the room to overflowing. As Minta walked to the sofa in front of the fire and sat down at one end, Chism sat at the other end.

"How I used to envy you," she said wistfully. Her smile faded as she stared into the orange flames.

Chism looked at her questioningly. "Envy *me*? That's crazy. Why would you envy me?"

"It's hard to explain, really," she said, still gazing at the fire. "I had a wonderful child-hood, loving parents, all the clothes and toys I could want."

"Like a yellow bike," said Chism, chuckling.

"Yes, a brand-new yellow bike. Which, by the way, I think was fabulous painted Passionate Purple."

"It was gross. But we're getting off the subject. Go back to what you were saying."

She turned her head to meet his gaze. "I envied you your permanence, Chism, the fact that you were accepted here, you belonged. The summer people are tolerated. There's a big difference there. I used to feel that I was spending my life visiting places, but never belonging anywhere."

He frowned. "Go on."

"I went to a private high school in upper New York State, where the majority of kids had been shipped in from all over the country. Yes, I went home every weekend, but at school it was . . . hard to bond with anyone, because I knew they'd all be going back to their own worlds. And each Christmas we went to Switzerland, where we were guests, visitors."

Chism nodded, his gaze riveted on her.

"Then every summer we'd come here, and I wasn't very old before I realized that the summer people were interlopers. We were tolerated, like I said, because we provided jobs for so many natives. But no matter how many generations of Westerlys come here, we'll never truly be part of Haven Port, because we'll never endure the hardship of the natives' lives."

She shifted to face him. "So, yes, I envied you, because you truly belonged here. It was yours. I adored going to your house, listening to your father tell his stories about his years on the whaling boats. I'd pretend that I lived on that side of the inlet, had roots there, just like you did." She shook her head. "I'm probably not making any sense."

"Yes, you are," Chism said slowly. "You are. I must admit, though, that I'm very surprised. You never said anything about this the summer we . . ." His voice trailed off.

"It was terribly confusing, Chism. I didn't know how to express it in words. I was so young then, still figuring out what life was all about. I realized I had so much. A huge closet full of clothes, more spending money than I needed, the prestigious address in Manhattan, an exclusive high school. Even with parents as wonderful as mine, though, I still felt a void. It was during that summer that I finally realized what it was. I wanted to really belong somewhere, like you did."

"Incredible." Chism got to his feet and walked to the fireplace, propping one arm on the mantel as he looked at her again. "You envied me. That was the summer I made up my mind that someday, somehow, I was going to have everything that your world offered. I told my father that, and he said I was wrong, that I should accept who I was, where I belonged, and not attempt to be what I wasn't."

"Life is so strange," said Minta, shaking her head. "We both viewed the other's existence as being the best one to have. Young minds, I suppose, falling prey to the grass-is-greener philosophy. But . . ." She hesitated.

"But?"

"The need to belong didn't go away as I grew older. That has suddenly become clear to me as I sit here saying all this aloud for the first time." The color drained from her face, and she ran a trembling hand through her hair. "My frantic drive to succeed in my career, to work myself into a state of total exhaustion, stems from that need to fit in, to be accepted. I'm a big shot at the advertising agency. Everyone knows me and I'm an intricate part of things."

"You belong."

"Yes. Dear heaven, all those years of pushing myself, telling myself I was loving every minute of the challenge. What I was, in actuality, is a very insecure woman."

She shook her head and forced a smile onto her lips. "That's just super. There's nothing like a little fireside analysis to force a person to take stock of her life. I have a feeling I'm a mental mess."

She strove for a lightness to her voice, but it didn't quite materialize. "So! What about you, Chism? Did you achieve your goals? Did you make big money, acquire all the materialistic things you were after?"

"Yes," he said, looking at her intently.

"And?"

"It was a hollow victory, Minta. A penthouse apartment, a foreign sports car, custom-tailored suits, original art, a stock portfolio, the whole nine yards. I have it all. But what am I supposed to do with it? I wander around my apartment realizing there's no one to talk to, no one to share with."

"And when you grew up here in Haven Port, there was always someone to talk to, who welcomed your company. Do you see how fortunate you were? How much you really had?"

"Yes, I guess I do. I'm a dozen years slow on the uptake, but it's sinking in now. My father was a very wise man, although I didn't realize that at nineteen. I loved him, but I left him. He was of another era, had old-fashioned ideas. I knew what I was going to go out and get, especially after you and I were no longer . . . Well, let's not get into that right now. What is this? Bare Your Soul Hour? This is serious stuff we're laying out here, Minta. A shrink would have a field day with this."

"I'm sure you're right. Chism, why are you here in Haven Port now, tending to things like your father did? Are you going to tell me again that it's none of my business?"

He looked at her for a long moment before he answered. "I'm here because I made a promise to my father before he died that I'd tend to the summer people one last time."

"I see. When—when did he die?"

"In the late spring, just before Memorial Day. He had a severe heart attack and wasn't allowed out of bed. I tried to convince him to come to San Francisco and live with me, but he refused. He wouldn't even listen to the idea of my staying in Maine, of him retiring and letting me move him to a better house. He was a proud man, proud of the work he had done all those years for all of you. He was comfortable with himself, at peace. Because of that, I made and kept my promise to him. That's why I'm here."

A single tear slid down Minta's cheek, and she dashed it away. "Thank you for telling me. Your father was a beautiful man."

"I had a problem with his outlook. I hate the class distinction here. My father simply accepted things the way they are. I despised it all then, and still do, but back then I had a very big chip on my shoulder. I decided I'd show them, by damn, that I was just as good as anyone else. I made it to the top, and now I wonder what in the hell I'm doing there."

"What exactly do you do for a living?"

"I'm a computer systems analyst. I custom-design computer systems to match the specific needs of a company. I latched onto computers in the army and knew I'd found my spot. The army, by the way, is where I went that summer when you and I . . . No, we're not touching that today." He paused, "Have you ever heard of a video computer game called *Power Climb*?"

"Goodness, yes. I own that game. The little gremlin moves through the mazes, gobbling up dollar signs that make him grow bigger. The aim is to get to the top of the maze, having all the money. If any of the bad guys catch him, he loses all his dollars and he's very small again. It's fun to play."

"It was my statement to society. Money is power. Without money you're nothing, out of the game. Class distinction simplified."

"You created *Power Climb*?"

"Yes, after I got out of the army. I was still very angry about—about a lot of things. It filled a need I had, then ended up making me a lot of money, which in turn gave me the freedom—and power—to start my own company. I had enough capital to hang on through the early years while I made a reputation for myself. I'm very selective about who I take on as clients."

"Oh?" said Minta, raising her eyebrows. "Do I hear a hint of class distinction, Mr. Talbert?"

"Why not? Lord knows I spent enough years taking it in the chops because I lived on the wrong side of the inlet."

"But you just said it was an empty victory, Chism, that your possessions aren't proving to be all that important."

He ran one hand over the back of his neck. "I know I said that, but . . ." He shook his head. "I'm in a strange mood, that's all. It's the storm, the feeling of being shut off from everything and being with someone . . . Forget it. You've said some things here today that surprised you too."

"I realize that. I suppose it is the storm, and . . . well, sharing inner thoughts with someone I've known for a long time. Someone I"—*loved*—"I . . ." She got to her feet. "Are you hungry? I'm ready for some dinner."

Chism stepped forward and gripped her upper arm. "You didn't finish your sentence. Someone who . . .?"

"You didn't finish yours, either. The truth of the matter is, I think we're both realizing that we divulged some very personal, very revealing facts to each other, and we're actually strangers."

The hell they were, Chism thought with a flash of anger. Maybe Minta thought she could forget that chapter in their lives of that long-ago summer, but it wasn't a closed book yet. Not until he had his answers.

He moved in front of her, lifting his hands to frame her face.

"Strangers, Miss Westerly?" he repeated softly. "Not even close. We know each other very well. Very well, indeed."

"Chism, don't. Leave the past alone. Let it go."

"For now. I'll put it on hold for now because this"—he slowly lowered his head toward hers—"is most definitely happening in the present."

No! Minta screamed silently.

Then all thought fled as Chism's mouth melted over hers.

Willow Hill
September 10, 1892

Dear Diary,
   Heat.
   How can I begin to explain how such an ordinary word has taken on an entirely new meaning for me?
   Heat.
   I repeat it over and over in my mind until it is no longer a word, but a living entity, that I could reach out to and touch.
   Dear diary, today I heard the voice of my wondrous blue-eyed gardener.
   The rain had stopped during the night, leaving everything fresh and sparkling this morning. Wearing my favorite dress, which in as green as the grass on the hill, I strolled

through the garden, gazing at the last of the brilliant late-blooming sweet peas.

From beneath my lashes, I stole quick glances at my gardener, watching him work, move, breathe; every motion he made tucked away as a cherished memory. At last I gathered my courage and stopped, my heart beating so rapidly it was actually painful. Praying there was enough breath left within me to speak, I said, "Good morning."

He straightened. He looked directly at me with those beautiful blue eyes, his sun-kissed hair in disarray. I saw the flash of anger, then it was gone and he spoke.

"Hello, Miss Masterson."

And then . . . the heat.

I can feel it anew even now, as I sit here in my bay window. It pulses within me, surrounding my heart, a sensation I've never known.

His voice is so deep and rich. It floated over me, caressing me like dark velvet. My name was not merely a name, but a melody more lovely than that which might be sung by the angels. His voice encircled my heart and touched my soul, the very essence of who I am.

I do believe I smiled then. Oh, I hope I smiled before nodding, and moving on. My knees were trembling terribly, and my cheeks were flushed from the bewildering heat that suffused me.

Oh, what am I to do? I yearn for tomorrow's dawn, which shall bring him to me once again. I have no patience with the wasted hours of this night, which stretch out before me cold and empty.

But, yet, what is the purpose of this journey my heart leads me on? My gardener is beyond my reach, not mine to have ever. Our worlds are too different, too far apart.

Oh, to be bold and defy convention, to speak again to my gardener and ask that he perhaps would care to stroll with me up the rise to sit beneath the young willow tree that grows there.

I would ask him his name, and listen to his deep voice as he tells me of his life, his dreams.

His hand might touch mine. His hands are tanned and look strong, yet his long, graceful fingers are gentle when he brushes the petals of the flowers.

I am so confused and frightened. I feel happy in one breath, then close to tears in the next. I am alive as I have never been, nearly bursting with energy, with the desire to live each moment to the fullest . . . with him.

What shall I do?
Sincerely,
Arminta Masterson.

Four

Willow Hill
September 5, 1990

Heat.

Chism's tongue parted Minta's lips, then delved deep into her mouth, drinking of her. Heat rocketed through him, arousing him instantly and enshrouding his mind in a hazy mist.

He couldn't think beyond the next beat of his thundering heart, because he was holding, kissing Minta. He pushed away the remembrance of what they'd just said to each other, the secrets that had surfaced, the truths they had acknowledged.

He'd deal with those later. Much later.

Minta clung to Chism as her knees began to tremble. She returned his kiss with all the passion she'd suppressed over the years. Inside her she felt the chill of confusion, of an emptiness in her life. And so she clung to Chism, welcoming his heat, drawing from his strength. She gave way to the desire pulsing madly within her, wishing only to feel, not to think.

She stroked his tongue boldly with hers. He groaned from deep in his chest and nestled her closer to his heavy arousal. He smelled deliciously of soap, fresh air, and man, and she wanted him with a burning need like none before.

As he dropped his hands from her face to her back, the heat from his fingers seemed to sear through her top. Her breasts were crushed to his chest in a sweet pain that heightened her passion even more. A sob caught in her throat as she threaded her fingers through his thick hair, urging his mouth harder onto hers.

Acting on instinct, obeying the driving need to possess this woman, Chism slid his hands beneath the waistband of her top. He caressed her smooth, heated skin, his hands roaming upward to her breasts, covered in the wispy lace of her bra. She eased away from him slightly, silently offering herself.

Groaning, he clamped one arm around her waist to hold her hips hard against his, then cupped her breast in his other hand. It was soft and full, and as his thumb stroked her, the nipple hardened, straining against the delicate lace.

The storm raging outside was insignificant compared to the fierce desire pounding through him. Minta, he thought dazedly. His Minta. His love, the only woman he'd ever loved. She was there now, where she belonged, with him. Minta, the only woman . . .

. . . *who had betrayed him.*

He stiffened and tore his mouth from hers. His hands dropped to his sides, and he stared down at her as she slowly opened her eyes. The desire he saw in their depths nearly broke his control.

"Chism?" she whispered. "Oh, Chism, I want you so much."

He gripped her hands and pulled them from his neck. As he released her, he stepped back, causing her to sway on her feet. He resisted the urge to reach out to her again.

"You want me?" he said, a raw and bitter edge to his voice. "For how long this time, Minta? Oh, I get it. You've figured out how to keep from dying of boredom during your monthlong stay here. Have a four-week fling with good ole Chism Talbert. Well, not this time, lady. I fell for your routine once, but I'm sure as hell not going to do it again. Find someone else to play with while you're stuck here."

The desire that had consumed Minta was extinguished so quickly, she felt as though she'd been doused with a bucket of cold water. Anger forged to the surface, and she planted tight fists on her hips.

"That is disgusting," she said, her voice quivering with fury. "How dare you insinuate that I'm playing some sort of sick game! I think it's time we thoroughly discussed that summer in the past, Chism. I'm getting very tired of your little zingers about how *I* was the one who caused everything to fall apart. Why don't we just lay it out on the table and be finished with it once and for all?"

Chism dragged a hand through his hair. "Oh, we'll discuss it, all right, but not now. I'm getting the hell out of here." He strode across the room.

"Chism, wait," she called. "The storm . . . It's dangerous out there."

He stopped and looked back at her. "It's dangerous in here too. At least I understand a New England storm and know what to expect. But you? You make up rules as you go along. I'll do well to remember that the bottom line is still the same. You're one of the summer people, Arminta, and I'm from the wrong side of the inlet. When it gets down to the crunch, you remember that and act accordingly. In short, Miss Westerly, you're a snob."

His heavy footsteps echoing through the house, he left, slamming the back door behind him.

Minta was so furious, the only sound she

was capable of making was a funny little squeak. She flung herself into a chair, then was on her feet again in the next instant, pacing back and forth in front of the fireplace. Her thoughts were fragmented, hurling at her from all directions.

She was *not* a snob . . . What purpose had there been to her life since graduating from college? Had her goals, her success, been nothing more than a deep-seated need to belong? . . . Chism had created *Power Climb*? But his achievements and financial rewards meant little to him, had been an empty victory? . . . Dear heaven, how she'd wanted him just minutes before, wanted to make love with him. . . . Why did he keep referring to the pain of that summer as being her fault? . . . Dammit, she was not a snob.

Minta stopped her pacing and sank onto the sofa, pressing her hands to her temples in an attempt to quiet the cacophony in her mind. Thunder boomed, and she quickly looked up.

Oh, Chism, she thought. He shouldn't have gone out into that storm, the idiot. Forget it, she told herself. She didn't care. Yes, she did, darn it. If he got injured, she'd . . . No, she couldn't even bear to think about the possibility. But what an infuriating man. He was driving her to the brink of insanity.

Weariness suddenly swept over her, and she sighed as she focused her gaze on the fire.

She shouldn't have come to Willow Hill, she

thought. She should have gone on a cruise, or to a sunny island where she could have spent hours lying on a warm, sandy beach. She should have gone to . . .

No. If she hadn't come to Willow Hill, she might have spent the remainder of her days living a life she was now forced to question. She had to determine if she really thrived in her fast-paced career and lifestyle, or was merely clinging to it for the sense of belonging it gave her.

Then there was the matter of Chism. The summer they'd shared should have been forgotten years before. The instant, burning desire that raged within her at the mere sight of him now, the sound of his voice, was a result of unfinished business, of unanswered questions left over from a time long past.

Okay, she thought, nodding decisively. She had her work cut out for her over the next month. She had to recuperate physically, reexamine her lifestyle and career, and get Chism Talbert totally out of her system once and for all.

With another weary sigh, Minta got to her feet and went into the kitchen to prepare herself a dinner that she had absolutely no appetite for.

At eight o'clock that night Minta sat curled up in the corner of the sofa, wearing a pale blue velour robe and totally engrossed in the thick, intriguing novel she was reading. The storm outside continued to rage, but she paid it little attention.

At eight minutes after eight, a bolt of lightning flashed so brightly, it lit up the living room. In the next moment the lights went out, leaving the fire as the only luminescence.

Minta pressed one hand to her wildly beating heart in an effort to calm it. She drew a steadying breath, then frowned in self-disgust.

It was not unusual for the electricity to go out during a storm in Haven Port. What was foolish was that she hadn't placed a flashlight or candles and matches within her reach on the end table next to her.

Her parents, she recalled, had always set those things out when a storm started. Minta, unfortunately, had never given them much thought. Now, she was alone, and for the life of her, she had no idea where the candles or a flashlight were kept. To top it off, there was only one small log left to add to the fire, which meant she would be without any light if she didn't get herself together.

She set the book aside and tentatively stood, her slippers making no sound as they touched the floor. Glancing around the room, she saw only darkness in all directions, beyond the small circle of light that the fire cast.

What she knew in her logical mind to be familiar pieces of furniture suddenly loomed in her imagination as beasts of prey, waiting to block her path and hurt her when she slammed into them.

"Oh, Minta, stop it," she said, then immediately wished she hadn't spoken aloud. Her voice revealed just how nervous she felt. In fact, she was close to being terrified, and her embarrassment over that did nothing to diminish her fear.

She inched her way forward, her arms stretched out before her, fingers spread. She probably looked like a robot who needed its joints oiled, she thought. A hysterical giggle caught in her tightening throat.

The rain clattered against the windows, sounding like the claws of monsters, scratching to get in. The wind howled with an eerie wail. Slowly, slowly, she walked toward the dining room, her hands sweeping the air for what might be in her path.

Candles, she reasoned, were in the kitchen, or the pantry beyond it, and all she had to do was cover the hundred miles between here and there. She was doing fine. She was—

"Oh!" she gasped as she collided with something solid. A sharp pain shot through one toe and up her leg.

With force born of fear her outstretched arms closed around an unknown something, and a moment later she heard the crunch. She had, she realized, just squished a lampshade.

Muttering several unladylike words, she

started off again, ignoring her throbbing toe. After what seemed like an eternity, she felt the kitchen door move under her palms, and pushed against it with a grateful sigh. She entered the kitchen, and it was, if possible, even darker than the living room and dining room.

Then she froze, a scream lodging in her throat.

A flickering light passed over the windows once, twice. It was the beam of a flashlight.

Someone was out there!

Had she locked the door? No, probably not. Despite all her years of living in New York City, she'd slipped back into the unlocked-door policy of Haven Port as easily as breathing.

Oh, Lord, she thought frantically. The light was getting brighter. He . . . it . . . the thing . . . was coming closer and closer. Don't panic, Arminta, she told herself. Too late—she was totally panicked.

No, she wasn't. She was going to defend herself, by gum. She hadn't lived in Manhattan for all this time for nothing. Hadn't she signed up for a self-defense class? Yes, sir, she certainly had. But, oh, darn, she'd been so busy, she hadn't attended one session.

And the light kept coming closer.

Minta edged away from the swinging door, sliding sideways as she kept her back against the wall, her trembling hands skimming along the smooth surface. Her eyes widened as her fingers touched . . .

Yes! It was the broom. She'd swept the kitchen floor after dinner, and hadn't yet returned the broom to the pantry.

As the back door began to creak open, she pressed her lips tightly together, her hands closed around the broom handle with a vise-like grip. The flashlight beam flickered over the floor, and a dark, undiscernible form moved with it.

Minta waited, hardly breathing, the echo of her racing heart roaring in her ears. She carefully, quietly raised the broom like a base-ball bat. Time dragged by with agonizing slowness as she forced herself to breathe.

A little farther, just a little bit . . .

She swung the broom with every ounce of her 115 pounds behind it, and hit her target with a satisfying and resounding thud.

She heard a muffled "Oomph," then the intruder was propelled through the swinging kitchen door, landing on the opposite side with a tremendous crash.

Minta rushed after him, still clutching her weapon. The flashlight had rolled halfway under the table, and she grabbed it. Broom in one shaking hand, the flashlight in the other, she turned the beam toward the floor.

"Ohmigod!"

Spreadeagled on his back on the floor was Chism Talbert.

At that moment the lights flickered on, dimmed once, then returned to full power. Minta continued to gape at Chism. He hadn't moved, or opened his eyes.

"Chism?" she whispered, leaning toward him. "Chism?"

He didn't move.

"Oh, mercy, what have I done?" Realizing she was still shining the flashlight directly in his face, she turned it off, then inched closer to him. "Hey!" she yelled. "Chism Talbert, quit acting like a jerk. I didn't hit you *that* hard. Besides, it's all your fault, because you scared the bejeebers out of me by skulking around in the dark like that."

He didn't move.

"You're making a puddle on the floor with your wet clothes and totally ruining the wax job. I mean it, Talbert, lying there like a dead body is not one bit cute." She paused and took a shaky breath, and her voice quivered when she spoke again. "Chism? Open your eyes, okay? Chism?"

He slowly raised his long, dark lashes and swept his gaze upward. He saw the broom Minta was still clutching and the expression of concern on her face. His eyes shifted back to the broom.

"Going for a ride?" he asked.

She blinked in surprise, opened her mouth, then snapped it closed again.

"Oh, good Lord," she said in the next breath, and burst into laughter.

It wasn't sophisticated, ladylike, twittery laughter; it was deep-from-the-belly, give-it-your-all laughter. The broom hit the floor with a clunk as she wrapped her arms around her stomach and howled.

Chism frowned, then struggled to his feet, his moan smothered by Minta's continued peals of laughter. Tears were forming in her eyes as she whooped, and despite his soreness, a smile crept onto his face. The smile reached his eyes, then broadened into a grin as he looked at Minta.

She was really something, he thought. She was beautiful, and her laughter was free and uninhibited. She laughed with the same total abandon that she made love with. That was Minta. His Minta.

And she'd socked him a good one, he mused, rubbing the small of his back. She hadn't cowered in a corner. She'd laid him out with a broom, for Pete's sake. Arminta Masterson Westerly was absolutely sensational.

"Excuse me, ma'am," he said, chuckling in spite of his effort not to. "Do you think you could possibly put a cork in it?"

"What?" Minta said merrily. "Oh." She took a gulp of air, then strove for a serious expression. She failed. Another bubble of laughter escaped from her lips before she could stop it.

She clamped a hand over her mouth. "There," she mumbled, her eyes sparkling, "all done."

"Is that weapon registered with the proper authorities?" he asked, pointing to the broom.

"Oh, don't start me off again," she said, her smile growing even bigger. "My stomach is killing me. Oh, my gosh, that was so funny, I can't believe it."

He gingerly rotated his neck back and forth. "I'd say it was a new interpretation of 'Wham, bam, thank you, ma'am.' You're a dangerous woman, Minta Westerly."

In more ways than one, he added silently. She was weaving her web around his heart again. Again? Had it ever really disappeared? No. She was just adding more strands and pulling them tighter. At the moment he didn't care. He should be keeping his defenses up, protecting himself, remembering the pain she'd caused him.

But he couldn't, not right now. Not when the sound of her laughter still seemed to echo in the air like wind chimes. Not when she looked soft and feminine in her blue robe. Not when the heat of desire was starting to coil within him.

"Chism," she said, forcing him to ignore his sensual thoughts, "what on earth were you doing sneaking around outside like a thief?"

"I remembered that the wood I split for you wasn't covered with a tarp, so I was bringing you some that was dry. Then the lights went out, and I wasn't sure if you were awake. You came here to rest, so for all I knew, you were in bed, not needing any more wood for tonight. Then I thought maybe you were awake, but didn't know where the candles were. So . . ." He shrugged.

"That was really very nice of you. I'm sorry I whacked you with the broom. I didn't hurt you, did I?"

"Only my pride," he said. "Although I expect a few bruises will show up tomorrow. You're a very scary lady."

"I was petrified."

His smile faded. "I apologize for frightening you. That wasn't my intention."

"No," she said. Her own expression became serious. "I know it wasn't. I appreciate your thinking of me, bringing the wood, and . . ." Her eyes filled with unexpected tears, which she attempted to blink away. "For heaven's sake, now I fall apart? That's ridiculous, except it has been a rather unsettling day."

He nodded. "We both discovered some startling facts about ourselves. The last thing you needed was to be scared out of your wits. I really am sorry, Minta. I'll unload the dry wood, then be on my way."

"No," she said quickly. "What I mean is, don't bother with the wood. You shouldn't be out in an electrical storm like this. I still have one log left, and that will be enough ·for tonight." Her glance slid over him. "You've spent most of this day soaking wet. You must be freezing."

He smiled slightly. "I could go through your father's entire wardrobe at this rate. I have his things at the house, and I'll bring them tomorrow. Dry wood too. I'll find a tarp to cover the other stack and—Dammit, Minta, you are so beautiful, so . . . I'd better go." He turned and started striding toward the kitchen.

"Chism, please, don't leave."

He stopped, his back to her. "I have to. If I stay, I'm going to take you in my arms and . . . I want you, Minta." He turned slowly to face her. "I want to make love with you. What happened in the past, the way that summer ended, should matter, should be keeping my anger at the boiling point. But right now, I don't give a damn about then. All I can think about is how much I ache for you."

"Yes," she said softly, "that's how I feel too. I suddenly have so much to deal with. The foundation of my life is crumbling, because I no longer know if I should be in the world I've created for myself. I could very well be there for the wrong reasons."

She sniffled, determined not to cry.

"But now," she went on, "in this little pocket of time and space that we're in, you're here. You're real, strong, solid. I need to lean on your strength, Chism, until I'm steady on my feet again. I want to make love with you, I truly do. Maybe it's wrong, maybe we're using each other, I don't know. But we could have this night with no regrets, no promises, just us stealing a precious moment of time, together."

"And tomorrow?" he asked. "What happens in the light of the new day?"

"Nothing. We won't talk about this, not even mention it. We'll each have memories to do with as we choose. I suppose that sounds brazen, but . . . I can't explain it, even to myself. I only know that for whatever reasons, it would be beautiful, and right."

Chism gazed at her for a long moment, warring with himself. Then he shoved the voice of rationality into a dusty corner of his brain and held out his hand to Minta.

"Come here," he said.

Willow Hill
September 12, 1892

Dear Diary,
    Together.
    My heart sings with joy, with the greatest happiness I have ever known.
    Where do I begin to put into words the glorious events of this miraculous day?
    Every minute, every second, is so precious that I think some details will have to remain as wondrous memories, or I shall find myself writing through the night and past dawn's light.
    His name is Joseph.
    Most people call him Joe, but I shall use Joseph, as it suits him far better. It is a strong, manly name, with a ring of dignity

and authority. It tastes like rich brandy on my lips. Joseph.

And we were together. Let me explain.

Mama and Papa announced at breakfast that they were to visit the Chamberlains today. I was invited, of course. I gathered every ounce of courage within me and pleaded a headache, asking to remain at home.

Mama was distressed, saying she would stay with me, as it is the cook's free day. I would be alone at Willow Hill, Mama told Papa, and that would never do. But Papa, bless him, puffed on his pipe and said I was perfectly safe here.

So, once alone, I obeyed a force more powerful than my sense of right and wrong and went to the garden. And he was there.

"Good morning," I said.

"Hello, Miss Masterson," he replied.

I sat on the bench beneath a nearby tree, arranged my skirt properly, then folded my hands in my lap.

"My name is Arminta," I said.

He straightened from his task of raking and looked directly at me. "That's a very pretty name," he said.

"Thank you. And you are?"

"Joseph, but people call me Joe."

"May I use Joseph?"

"If you like. Was there something you wanted?"

"Just to talk . . . Joseph. Am I disturbing you? I'll leave if you prefer."

"I can work and talk. I doubt your parents would approve of your being here, though. I saw them go off in the buggy."

"This day is mine," I said.

"And you want to spend it talking to me?"

"Yes."

"Then we'll talk, together . . . Arminta."

Oh, dear diary, has there ever been such a lovely word as "together"?

Joseph worked, I watched, and we talked. I heard his anger at times, and he spoke fiercely of what he is determined to do with his life, how he will succeed in his goal to have wealth. He vows to never again be looked down upon, as he is now by the summer people who come to Haven Port.

Several times, he smiled, and his smile was like sunshine bursting through the dark clouds.

Once he laughed, and it was a glorious sound. I told him of my inability to do needlepoint, and he laughed, just as I did.

"How will you ever fit properly into society?" he said. "No talent for needlepoint? You are a disgrace."

"I know," I said happily. "But I'm a spinster, you see, so my disgrace is already established. There is no hope for me, I fear."

"You don't want to marry?"

"I wish more than just to marry," I said. "It's

difficult to explain, and I don't expect any-one to understand."

"I understand, Arminta," he said quietly, "because I want more from life than some think I should have."

The hours flew by as we talked on and on. I made a lunch, and we shared it sitting on that bench beneath the tree.

Then far too soon, in the late afternoon, I heard the jingle of bells on the horse's har-ness, and knew my parents were returning.

"I must go, Joseph," I said. "Thank you for a lovely day."

"The pleasure was mine."

And then . . . he took my hand, lifted it to his lips, and lightly kissed my shaking fin-gers.

That strange heat rushed through me, and I feared I would swoon at his feet.

His lips were warm and soft, and I can feel them still where he brushed them across my fingers.

"Good-bye, Arminta," he said, "until the next time we're together."

"Good-bye, Joseph."

Together.

I yearn for that moment, I ache for it to come. Together with Joseph.

Good night.

Sincerely,

Arminta Masterson

Five

Willow Hill
September 5, 1991

Together.

She and Chism were together, Minta thought, as she moved into his embrace. He felt so good, and smelled so good, and she was aware of a comforting sense of coming home, of being where she was meant to be.

She refused to think. Her life was in such sudden turmoil, she couldn't deal with it all. This night, this stolen night, belonged only to her and Chism.

He lowered his head and captured her lips, and she sighed in contentment, giving herself up totally to the desire swirling within her.

Was he a fool? Chism asked himself. Hell, he didn't know, or care. Not tonight. He wasn't going to dwell on anything except the woman in his arms, and what they were about to share.

The kiss deepened, and reality was pushed further into the shadows. Chism's hands roamed restlessly over Minta, across her back, down to the slope of her buttocks, then upward again to her breasts. Blood pounded in his veins, and his manhood surged with need for her.

He lifted his head for a moment to draw a raspy breath, then his mouth sought hers again in a kiss that was suddenly urgent, hungry, filled with passion now out of control. And Minta responded in kind.

Forcing himself to end the kiss, Chism led her into the living room, to the rug in front of the fireplace, flicking off lamps as he went. He paused long enough to lay the last log on the flames, then turned to her once more.

Their eyes met, speaking of memories of days long past and a desire new and mature. All was familiar, vividly remembered, and so wondrous.

Chism shed his clothes, then stood in the glow of the firelight. Minta's gaze skimmed his body, seeing the changes from boy into man in the corded muscles, the obvious strength and power. She looked into his dark eyes once more and, smiling, dropped her robe to the floor.

Then it was Chism's turn to gaze at every

inch of her, the slender yet womanly body replacing his memory of the girl.

"You are exquisite," he murmured. "You were lovely then, but now you're beautiful beyond words, Minta."

"So are you, Chism," she said softly. "The boy is gone. The man is magnificent."

They each took one step forward, closing the distance between them and erasing as well the years that had separated them.

Lips touched, bodies touched, and their passions soared even higher. They sank to the rug to lie close, to rediscover what they'd once known so intimately, and to explore the bounty of the new. Hands, lips, and tongues were never still as they both claimed again what once had been theirs.

Chism dipped his head to draw one of Minta's breasts deep into his mouth, suckling, savoring, laving the nipple to a taut bud. He moved to the other breast, and a sigh of pure pleasure whispered from her lips.

She trailed the finger of one hand through the dark, moist hair on his chest, and his body jerked when she found one nipple buried there.

As his mouth continued to pay homage to her breasts, her hand crept lower, lower, seeking and finding all that declared him man.

He lifted his head, and his eyes were smoldering with desire.

"I want you, Chism Talbert," she said, her

voice trembling. "I never stopped wanting you."

He kissed her once more, a deep, mind-drugging kiss, then moved his body over hers.

"You're mine, Minta Westerly," he said roughly. "You always have been."

"Yes."

He thrust within her, joining their bodies, driving deep. She received him joyfully, loving all that he brought to her. As he moved within her, she matched his rhythm, first slow then faster, harder, gloriously real.

They were hurled backward in time to a summer of love, of dreams, of youthful joy. But they were in the present as well, taking the best of both worlds with them as they soared on passion's wings to a place created just for them. Together.

"Chism!"

"Oh, yes. Yes, Minta, now. Now."

A heartbeat apart, they reached the summit of their flight and burst into wonder. They clung to each other, savoring the shuddering spasms consuming them.

The last ripples of ecstasy swept through them, then quieted, leaving them sated and content. Chism rolled onto his back, taking Minta with him, their bodies still joined as she lay stretched out on top of him. He held her close as she nestled her head on his broad chest.

Hearts slowed to normal tempos, their bodies cooled, but neither one moved, or spoke, not wishing to break the spell of magic.

Oh, yes, Minta thought dreamily, it was still there, the magic. But now it was magnified tenfold by what they had just shared. Only with Chism, only then and only now, had she felt such magic.

This was lovemaking as it was meant to be, could only be, with Chism. Her heart had spoken the truth years ago—she was in love with Chism Talbert.

Despite the pain he had caused her, and the tears that had flowed for so long, her love never totally died. Now, she realized, it had been rekindled to burn even brighter, with the added ingredients of experience and maturity.

Yet what was she going to do? This was to have been stolen time, the memory of one night to cherish. They had agreed on that, so Chism would never know that she still loved him.

She sighed and closed her eyes.

Chism turned his head to gaze into the leaping flames of the fire, his hold on Minta tightening. She was his, he thought. The women he'd been with over the past dozen years meant nothing. The lovemaking he'd just shared with Minta had been incredibly beautiful, erasing time and distance, connecting the past to the present.

He loved her.

He now knew that he had never stopped loving her. He'd used the anguish of her betrayal as a wall around his heart, to keep at bay what he could no longer deny. He had been in love with Arminta Masterson Westerly since he was nineteen years old.

He was older this time, though, and wiser. He knew how to protect himself. This time, dammit, he wasn't setting himself up for heartache. This time he would keep silent. Minta would not know how he felt.

"Are you falling asleep?" he asked quietly.

"Mmm. I could very easily. That was wonderful, Chism, so special."

"Yes."

"You're not sorry this happened, are you?"

He hesitated a moment. "No. Are you?"

"No. We're adults, consenting adults. This was our night of—of magic. There's nothing wrong with that because we both agreed to steal this night out of time. I have no regrets."

They were silent for several minutes, lost in their own thoughts.

"Minta," Chism said finally, "I'd better leave. The storm is about over, I think. The fire is burning low, and you're going to get chilled."

"You could stay, Chism. This is still our special night."

"No, I don't think that's a good idea."

He gripped her waist and gently lifted her off him. As he reached for his clothes, Minta stared at him, but was unable to read the expression on his face. She slipped her robe on, then stood. Chism stood, too, dressing quickly.

"Well, good night," he said awkwardly. *Dammit, I love you, Minta.*

I love you, Chism Talbert. "Good night."

He lifted one hand as though to touch her face, then curled the fingers into a fist and strode from the room.

Minta wrapped her hands around her upper arms and watched him go. Then she sank onto the edge of the sofa, covered her face with her hands, and cried.

She cried because she didn't have the energy left to fight the tears. She cried because the very foundation of her world had crumbled beneath her. She cried because she was in love with a man who didn't love her, and the future stretched before her like a dark, empty, lonely road.

At last the tears slowed. She sank against the back of the sofa, drew a deep breath, and allowed her arms to fall with an exhausted thud on either side of her.

"Well, Minta?" she said, staring up at the ceiling. "Now what?"

She'd had a good, womanly weep, she mused, a healthy, cleansing cry. The next step was to gather her wits about her and figure out what in heaven's name she was going to do about this mess.

For two cents, she thought dryly, she'd

crawl into bed, pull the blankets over her head, and not emerge for at least ten years.

Forget that, she thought in the next instant. She was an Arminta, by gum. The Armintas who had gone before her had been women of courage, intelligence, and fortitude. They had been survivors, winners, and she would be too.

Feeling more confident, she got to her feet. As she turned toward the stairs, she saw the crunched lampshade. A bubble of laughter escaped from her lips, and gave the shade a friendly pat as she passed it.

"Poor baby," she said. "You look like I feel."

But she would *not* be defeated by her woes, she vowed. She'd figure everything out. Somehow. She would be true to the Armintas of the past, and those yet to come.

Somehow.

Willow Hill
September 15, 1892

Dear Diary,
 Secrets.
 They are a part of me now, an extension of who I am. I have always been open and honest with my parents, but that time is behind me as I move further into my world of secrets. My world of Joseph.
 For I am in love. For all time, forever, I shall love my Joseph.
 Three days have passed since I put words on this paper, but I have been in such a state of confusion, it was impossible to thread sentences together. Now, at last, the tangled web has unraveled to reveal to me the truth of my love.
 I have grown bolder with each passing

day, caring not who observes me on the bench in the garden talking with Joseph as he works. I have expected Mama and Papa to call me to task, but they have said nothing of my rash behavior. What are they thinking? When shall they demand that I conduct myself with proper decorum?

But enough of my ramblings. It is Joseph, beautiful Joseph, who is at the center of my mind and heart.

Today, after spending the afternoon in the garden, I bid Joseph good-bye and walked alone up the hill to sit beneath the willow tree.

It was so peaceful there. I was somewhat chilled from the wind, but I ignored the slight discomfort and gazed across the inlet. Joseph lives on the other side with his parents and two sisters, and I wondered which of the small bungalows was his home.

And then . . . my heart races at the memory . . . then Joseph appeared beside me beneath the willow tree. He didn't speak, or smile. He was just suddenly there. He sat next to me, placed one hand on my cheek, and kissed me.

There are not words to describe how glorious that kiss was. I wish to keep no secrets from you, dearest diary, as I must from my parents, but I am not capable of expressing the wondrous sensation of Joseph's lips on mine.

When he ended the kiss, he looked deep into my eyes and said, "You have stolen my heart, Arminta Masterson. I love you."

Tears filled my eyes, silly tears of joy, and my voice quavered when I spoke.

"And I love you, Joseph."

He kissed me again, then once more, before rising and saying it was too cold for me to tarry longer, and I should go home.

"Until tomorrow, my love," he said.

Oh, I am consumed with happiness so exquisite, it is almost painful.

I refuse, this night, to dwell on the future, to question what is to become of me, of Joseph, and of how we feel. Love has touched my heart and soul, and this night it is mine to savor and cherish.

I shall sleep now, and I know I shall dream of Joseph and the ecstasy of our kisses.

Good night.

Sincerely,

Arminta Masterson

Six

Willow Hill
September 9, 1991

Secrets.

Minta hung up the kitchen telephone, but did not immediately remove her hand from it.

Secrets, she thought, staring across the room at nothing. She was suddenly filled to overflowing with them. She'd just assured her mother over the phone that she was resting and eating properly, just as the doctor ordered. Everything was fine, and it was delightful to be back at Willow Hill, spending her days in such a relaxing environment.

Ha! thought Minta, picking up her coffee mug and crossing the room to the table. It had been three days since she'd spoken to Chism, but the remembrance of their lovemaking was as vivid as if it had just happened.

The mere thought of that night sent her desire for him soaring. She was in love with Chism Talbert, and that love seemed to intensify with every beat of her heart.

She drained her mug, then wandered aimlessly into the living room.

She adored this house, she mused. She always had. The library off the living room was one of her favorite places to spend time. What a marvelous office it would make, with its bookshelves, fireplace, and big windows that allowed the sunshine to pour in. In the winter she would have a spectacular view of the snowy fairyland outside, while a warming fire crackled on the hearth.

She entered the library and pictured herself working there, doing free-lance assignments for prestigious advertising firms. In the spring she could plant a garden, then reap the rewards of fresh vegetables and lovely flowers.

She would have a dog, she mentally rambled on. She'd always wanted a dog, and a kitten too. She'd get them at the same time, so they'd grow up together and be friends. She'd fill her days with rewarding, challenging work, and her evenings with reading all the wonderful books she'd never had time to enjoy.

But after the evening, she thought, came the night, the trek up the stairs to bed . . . alone. Without Chism. He would be leaving

Haven Port soon, and that would be that. Chism Talbert would walk out of her life forever.

Minta sighed. Was she crazy for even day-dreaming about quitting her job? Would she stagnate there at Willow Hill, bored and desperately lonely? Would she turn into an eccentric spinster, who lived only for the memories of a lost love?

Oh, for Pete's sake, she admonished herself, how melodramatic. Haven Port wasn't at the end of the earth. She could make trips into Manhattan to see her parents and friends, to attend concerts and plays. Then, instead of being caught up in the city's frantic pace, she would return to Willow Hill and the rejuvenating peace it offered her. She would have the best of both worlds, everything she needed and wanted.

Except Chism Talbert.

"Arminta, shut up."

Whatever decisions she reached about the future, they had to be separate and apart from any thought of Chism. She was facing the unsettling realization that for years she'd been attempting to create a sense of belonging. She had to look deep within herself to discover who she really was, what would bring her true happiness, what life would be right for her.

A life that did not include Chism.

She walked slowly back through the house toward the kitchen, imagining herself there day after day, and smiling when she wondered if she'd ever be able to master needlepoint.

A knock at the back door brought her from her thoughts. As she crossed the kitchen, she knew without any doubt that she would open the door to find Chism standing there.

He was, and as she smiled up at him, she noticed he definitely was not smiling at her.

"Hi and good morning," she said cheerfully. "Come in, Chism. Heavens, it's nippy out there, isn't it?"

He narrowed his eyes and entered the house. "You're very chipper," he said gruffly.

"Well, there's no reason not to be," she said, shrugging. Would he notice if she flung herself into his arms and kissed the living daylights out of him? Oh, mercy, how she loved this man. "Coffee?"

"No. I've had plenty this morning. The dock is finished."

"Oh. Did you bring a bill so that I can write you a check?"

"I haven't figured out the cost yet." Lord, she was gorgeous, he thought. He wanted to take her into his arms and—Forget it, Talbert. "Listen, there are late blueberries down by the inlet. I thought you might want to pick them before they're lost to a frost."

"Marvelous. I'll go right now." She hesitated a moment. "Would you care to join me?"

Not a chance, Chism thought. He wasn't spending any time with Arminta Masterson

Westerly. He was putting as much distance between them as possible. Maybe he couldn't do anything about loving her, but he sure as hell wasn't going to torture himself by being close to her.

"Chism?" she asked, puzzled by the peculiar expression on his face. "Do you want to pick blueberries?"

"Yeah, okay." Oh, great, Chism thought. He was now certifiably insane. "Do you have a pail? You'll need your jacket too."

"I'll be ready in a jiffy. Oh, fresh blueberries. My mouth is watering already. Should we have them with cream? Or I could make a cobbler, and we'll eat the whole thing hot from the oven. Yummy. I'll get my jacket."

She hurried from the room, and Chism shook his head in confusion. "We," she had said, as though it was the most natural thing in the world that they'd share the blueberries once they'd picked them.

He was probably reading too much into her chatter, he decided. The problem was that it had sounded so right, the way it should be. *We.* And if they didn't come and cart him away to the funny farm, he'd voluntarily commit himself. He was definitely out of his mind.

The day had a clean, crisp feel to it. Autumn was in the air, with the whisper of winter close on its heels.

Minta filled her lungs with the tangy scent of saltwater as they walked up the hill at the back of the Westerly property.

"No exhaust fumes, no smelly buses," she said. "No honking of horns and no people jostling and yelling. I think I'm in culture shock."

"You must miss New York City, all the activity."

"No," she said thoughtfully, "I don't. It was habit, not happiness, that kept me there. Plus, that nifty little bomb my subconscious allowed to surface the other day."

"About needing to feel that you belong? Is that troubling you?"

"Yes, of course it is. I have to reevaluate everything, discover what I should really be doing and where I should be doing it. I had this thought that I could . . ." She hesitated, uneasy at speaking her new dream aloud. "Well, live at Willow Hill and do free-lance work. I'm very good at my profession, and have an excellent reputation for original concepts."

Chism stopped walking. "You're actually thinking about moving to Willow Hill permanently?"

She halted and turned to look at him. "It has possibilities."

He folded his arms over his chest. "Come on, Minta, who are you kidding? You said yourself when you arrived that you were dreading every minute of being here and having nothing to do. I'd be surprised if you lasted the month that your doctor insisted you take off." He shook his head. "You're not a Mainer, a person who could live here year round. You just don't have the personality, the temperament, for it."

"Oh, is that so?" she said, her voice rising. "You certainly are quick to pass judgment, Chism Talbert. How does it feel to be so worldly and wise? You don't even really know me."

He looked at her for a long moment, and his voice was very low when he spoke again.

"Don't I? I'd say that I know you very well, Miss Westerly."

A warm flush stained Minta's cheeks as a picture of what had transpired on the living-room rug flashed before her eyes.

Damn him, she thought, he was making sexual innuendos, shifting the conversation into forbidden territory. And her body was responding. Well, she had no intention of standing there and allowing Chism Talbert to push her sensual buttons.

"Forget it, Chism," she said. "I'm sorry I even brought the subject up." She turned and stalked off.

Chism quickly followed and gripped her arm, forcing her to stop again. She glared at him, at his hand on her arm, then met his gaze once more. He dropped his hand to his side.

"Okay, okay," he said, "that was a cheap shot, and I apologize." He dragged one hand through his hair. "Seriously, Minta, you're not really contemplating living here, are you?"

"Yes, I am," she said, lifting her chin. "It's none of your business, Chism, but I seem to have a penchant for baring my soul to you. I've done a great deal of thinking these past few days. I've come to realize that the life I lead no longer holds much appeal. I'm tired, not just physically, but mentally and emotionally as well. It's time for a change, and Willow Hill might be the answer."

"You *are* serious," he said incredulously.

"I certainly am. Ironic, isn't it? You'll be leaving here soon, and I just may stay on. You'd be the visitor if you ever returned, and I'd be the native. As a matter of fact, why are you still here? You've fulfilled your promise to your father. If you're hanging around to close up Willow Hill, don't bother. I'm sure you have important things to do in . . . Where did you say you lived? Oh, yes, San Francisco. You must be eager to get back there."

No, he wasn't, Chism thought, because he didn't really have anything to go back to. Minta wasn't the only one who'd done a lot of thinking, and the conclusions he'd come to were far from comforting.

His life was empty and cold. He had a great many acquaintances, but few friends. The women he dated when he wasn't working fourteen-hour days were simply to have a good time with, no one to fall in love and build a home with.

"No comment?" Minta shrugged. "I'm going to pick blueberries." She spun around and marched away.

Chism watched her for a minute, then followed slowly behind her.

Minta Westerly a permanent resident of Willow Hill? he mentally repeated. No, it didn't fit. She was Old Money, accustomed to the finest the world could offer. But then again, she'd obviously worked very hard at her career. She hadn't sat back and waited for her wealthy parents or a wealthy husband to hand her everything on a silver platter.

Maybe she was right, he mused. Maybe he didn't know Minta very well at all. The Minta he knew was eighteen years old—and had nearly destroyed him with her betrayal. Leopards didn't change their spots. Minta was Minta. Putting aside the fact that he still loved her, the time had come to demand an explanation for what she had done to him.

Minta was busily picking blueberries, dropping them in her pail, when he reached her. He picked a few berries, popped them into his mouth, then shoved his hands into the back pockets of his jeans.

"We ate a lot of these that last summer," he said.

Her head snapped around, and she looked up at him. "Yes, we did."

A muscle ticked in his tightly clenched jaw. "I have one question for you, Minta. Why? Why did you do it? Who got to you? Your parents? Or did you yourself realize what you were sacrificing? I know that summer is old news, but it's unfinished business. I want to know why."

Her eyes widened. "*You're* asking *me*? My God, Chism, that's *my* question to ask, don't you think?"

He frowned. "Not even close. Dammit, I loved you, and you said you were in love with me. We had it all worked out, all our plans made. That night, that last night, we were leaving together. We were going to get married, and . . . I waited for you. I stood there for hours waiting, telling myself you'd come to me, that we'd have a wonderful life together. But, damn you, you never showed up."

"What?" she whispered.

"I should have known I was being a fool, that one of the summer people would never lower herself to marry a Mainer from the wrong side of the inlet. All I want to know is why. Why didn't you have the decency to tell me the truth, tell me it was just a summer fling to you? You betrayed me, Minta, and I've never understood why."

"No," she said, stepping back from him. You're wrong, Chism. I came to your house just as we planned. I had my suitcase with me, and I'd left a note for my parents telling them that I was in love with you and was going to marry you. Dammit, Chism, I came to you."

"No," he said, though his face had paled. "My father told me you'd come by earlier and said to meet you under the willow tree, instead of at the house. He gave me some money, told me to have a wonderful, happy life with you. I was there for hours, at the tree, waiting."

"Dear heaven," she breathed. "I went to your house. Your father hugged me, said he was sorry, but you'd left town that afternoon. He said you were probably going to join the army. I couldn't believe it. My heart was breaking, and I could hardly see through my tears as I ran home and snuck back into the house. Everything we'd shared had meant nothing to you, nothing. We, my family, left for New York the next day right on schedule. I told them I wasn't feeling well, when in actuality I was shattered, moving in a haze of pain. *You* betrayed *me*, Chism."

"No. No, I didn't!" he exclaimed, his mind racing. "Oh, Lord, it fits, it all fits. My father kept telling me not to try to be what I wasn't, try to have what wasn't meant to be mine. All summer he'd make remarks about how he loved me and would do anything to keep me from being hurt. I shrugged it off, ignoring him for the most part. I said I could take care of myself. I can remember one time he said how much he liked you, how lovely you were, what a joy it was to see you smile. But . . ." He drew a shuddering breath.

". . . but when he said that, he added that some worlds just aren't meant to mesh, some things aren't meant to be. I dusted it off as more of his ramblings. Yet when you didn't come to the willow tree . . . I left Haven Port the next day too. I joined the army and made up my mind that never again would anyone look down on me because of what I wasn't, for what I didn't have."

Tears filled Minta's eyes. "I didn't do that, Chism. I loved you so much. The prejudice didn't come from my side of the inlet, it came from yours. Your father didn't want us to be together. Yes, he liked me as a person, but he didn't want his son to marry one of the summer people. He must have felt I didn't belong in your world, and that I would never make you happy. It was your father who kept us apart, destroyed our plans for our future. *I* was the one who didn't measure up to standards, not you. All these years I thought . . ." She shook her head as a sob choked off her words.

Feeling close to tears himself, Chism stared at Minta. She met his gaze, and they each relived the anguish of that fateful night. Slowly, painfully, they accepted the truth, yet that truth shook them to the very core of their beings.

"I need—I need to be alone right now," Minta finally whispered. "I just . . . I can't . . ."

She whirled around and ran up the incline, knocking over the pail, spilling blueberries across the ground.

Chism watched her go, his vision blurred by tears. He drew one hand over his eyes, then looked up at the heavens.

"Dad," he said, his voice raspy, "I know you thought you were doing the right thing, but . . ."

He shook his head, looking again up the hill, but Minta was gone. A chilling wind swirled around him, rustling the low bushes, and his attention was caught by the blueberries that had fallen from Minta's pail.

That was how he felt. Just like those blueberries, scattered across the ground, not knowing how to make himself whole again.

Willow Hill
September 21, 1892

Dear Diary,
    Tears.
    I have wept so many tears during this seemingly endless week of loneliness. They are ridiculous tears, I readily admit, but no amount of scolding my puffy-eyed, red-nosed reflection in the mirror halts their flow.
    Mama has expressed concern over my appearance, and I lie once more, the untruths now pouring from my lips like a rushing river.
    I am apparently allergic, I told Mama, to the autumn grass growing in Maine. I have only now discovered my adversity to it, as we have never before stayed at Willow Hill beyond Labor Day.

Thus, I must now twice daily rest, says Mama, with muslin pads filled with wet tea leaves pressed against my swollen eyes.

Why do I weep?

Because Joseph has gone to Boston with his father to purchase winter supplies. It has been nearly a week since he kissed me good-bye time and again beneath the willow tree, and told me his thoughts would be only of me during his absence.

"I love you, my Arminta, my beloved," he said, holding me tightly in his arms.

"And I love you, darling Joseph," I replied, smiling through my tears.

This week of misery has made me realize that life without Joseph, without his love, would be empty and cold, too unbearable to endure.

Memories of the precious moments spent with him are not enough to sustain me. The memories are mine, and I shall cherish each one, but to be truly happy I must be with Joseph through the remaining days of my life.

He speaks often of his plans for a better life, of leaving Haven Port and working to become a successful man of wealth and power. And now as he talks he says that we shall have a fine home and servants to do our bidding.

No, he has not officially asked for my hand in marriage, but ours is not a conventional relationship. There is no point in him speaking privately with Papa, for consent to our union would never be granted.

Joseph and I are of different worlds, but of this we care nothing. Our love is the only matter of importance.

And so, diary dear, the "we" Joseph speaks of is understood between us as the way it is, the way it must be, if there is to be sunshine in either of our lives.

How bold I am to write with such determination to defy convention. How changed I am from the girl who arrived at Willow Hill at the beginning of summer. I am a woman in love, and have discovered strengths within myself that I did not know I possessed.

The only shadow on the horizon of my future is the knowledge of the sorrow I shall cause Mama and Papa when I tell them of my love for Joseph, and my plans to become his wife.

My tears flow once more as my aching heart yearns for Joseph's return, for his smile and touch, for the glorious ecstasy of his lips against mine.

I shall sleep now, my diary, put one more day behind me, and have one less to endure without Joseph.

Soon, he will return to me, and when he does, there will be no more tears.

Good night.

Sincerely,

Arminta Masterson

Seven

Willow Hill
September 15, 1991

Tears.

She was a living, breathing, walking, talking waterfall of tears, Minta thought with disgust. In the week since she'd learned the devastating truth of Chism's father's deception, she'd cried more tears than she had in her entire life.

Sighing, she placed a pan of corn bread in the oven, then set the timer on the back of the stove. Over and over, she'd relived that scene by the blueberry bushes. Emotions had slammed into her with staggering force during the following days and nights. Emotions of disbelief, anger, sadness, loneliness, and, worst of all, a sense of years lost forever, stolen from her.

"Enough is enough, Arminta," she said as she poured herself some apple juice.

Learning the truth of what had happened in the past didn't change the harsh reality of the present. She still loved Chism, and he hadn't expressed one word of love for her. He would be leaving Haven Port soon, and might have left already, since she hadn't seen him or heard from him during the past week.

What had he been thinking, she wondered, since that day by the blueberry bushes? Had he simply shrugged it off, said, "Well, I'll be damned, it was my father who was the spoke in the wheel," and put the whole scenario from his mind? Was it now finished business?

Minta narrowed her eyes. Finished business? Not for her, it wasn't. If Chism had left Haven Port, then that, she supposed, was that. But if he was still there . . .

The timer on the oven shrilled, startling her so much that her hand jerked, splashing apple juice down the front of her sweatshirt.

"Cute," she said, pulling the sticky material away from her skin. "I adore your eau de cologne, Arminta."

Chism flung his pencil onto the mass of papers strewn on the top of his kitchen table.

Tilting the chair back onto two legs, he closed his eyes and squeezed the bridge of his nose.

He had another headache. No, correct that. It was the *same* headache he'd been plagued with ever since that scene by the blueberry bushes with Minta a week ago. His mind never seemed to quiet as he chased unsettling facts around and around in his tired brain.

Answers to twelve-year-old questions had led to even more questions, which encompassed virtually every aspect of his life. And right smack-dab in the middle of the mess was Arminta Masterson Westerly.

With each endless day and restless night, he'd been taunted by the realization that Minta had not betrayed him that night long ago. He could envision her so clearly, standing there in the living room, clutching her suitcase as her hopes and dreams, her faith in him and their love, were shattered by his father's words.

He could see her crying, not wishing to believe that his declarations of love and all that they had shared had meant nothing. Ernest Talbert had done what he felt was best, but two young hearts had been broken because of it.

Chism opened his eyes and stared at the papers on the table. He'd attempted to bury himself in work this past week, and was supposed to be preparing a computer program that would meet the needs of an import-export company in San Francisco. But his head ached, his mind was mush, and he'd accomplished little.

One burning question kept hammering at him, screaming louder than the others: What in the hell was he still doing in Haven Port, Maine?

A knock at the front door brought him from his tangled thoughts, and he thudded the chair back onto four legs, doubling the pain in his throbbing head in the process. His steps heavy, he strode to the door and flung it open.

Then he knew, without a doubt, why he was still in Haven Port.

"Minta," he said.

"Hello, Chism," she said quietly. "I thought perhaps you'd gone back to San Francisco."

"No, I . . . No." He stepped aside. "Come in."

She entered the house, and he closed the door behind her as she walked slowly into the living room. When she reached the center of the small room, she turned to face him.

"This house holds a lot of memories," she said. "It's not the same without your father here, though. I can see him so clearly in my mind, sitting there in his favorite chair." She paused. "Chism, I think we should talk."

"What about?" he asked, remaining by the door, ordering himself not to move. It took every ounce of self-control he possessed not to gather her to him, hold her and kiss her, erase the pain of that summer night.

"May I sit down?" she asked.

"Sure."

Minta settled onto the sofa, then looked at him over her shoulder. He crossed to the easy chair that was the farthest away from her, which in the small room wasn't very far. He propped one ankle on the other knee, and strove for what he hoped was a bland expression.

"Chism," she said, "this has been a long, difficult week for me. Once I really comprehended what had happened that summer, I thought I could put it all to rest. You appear to be very calm and relaxed."

No, he thought, he was just a good actor.

"So, I'd appreciate it," she continued, "if you'd humor me a bit, talk about what actually happened."

He lifted one shoulder in a shrug. "Whatever."

She frowned. "You are a cool customer. You were hell-bent on demanding to know why I 'betrayed' you that night. Now that you've learned the truth, you've apparently put the entire thing from your mind."

He didn't speak. He just looked at her, no readable expression on his face.

"Fine," she said, throwing up her hands. "I envy you the ability to just forget it. Well, I can't seem to do that, Chism, so the hell with my pride, because I need to talk this through. You can sit there like a block of wood, I really don't care, but I'll have my say."

"Go right ahead."

"I want you to know that I'm not angry at your father for what he did, because I believe that he did it out of love. But, Chism, I can't seem to stop wondering what life would have been like if we'd been allowed to do what we planned. I can't help feeling that years were stolen from us, years that can't be replaced."

She paused to draw in a deep breath, and he still remained silent.

"I thought," she went on, "if we talked, sorted it out, we—*I* might come to realize that it was all for the best, that we were too young and marriage between us would have been a disaster. I can't seem to get that message across to myself. Obviously, you have, so I'm asking you to help me to put it to rest, so I can get on with my life."

"I can't do that," he said.

She leaped to her feet. "Damn you, Chism Talbert, do you think coming here was easy for me? My pride is in shreds. I'm a mature woman, but I can't handle the emotions tearing at me. Okay, fine, forget it. If you won't share your thoughts on why it was all for the best, then I'll figure it out for myself." She lifted her chin. "I'm sorry I bothered you."

"Minta, sit down. Please."

She sank back onto the sofa. Chism dropped

his foot to the floor and leaned forward, resting his elbows on his knees. "I can't tell you that what my father did was the proper thing for us, that he saved us from making a terrible mistake. I can't say that, Minta, because—because I'm not convinced that it's true."

Her eyes widened. "What?"

"Ah, hell." He stared up at the ceiling, then met her gaze again. "I'm not angry at my father, either, Minta, but I know that what happened that night changed the entire course of my life, my attitudes, my dreams. . . . When I take an inventory of who I am, I'm not thrilled with what I find. Stolen years? Yes, that sums it up very well."

He shifted back in the chair, his hands flat on his thighs. "Minta, why did you make love with me the other night?"

Because I love you, you nincompoop, she thought. "We're not discussing that," she said. "Besides, we didn't make love, per se. We—we had sex. There's a tremendous difference between the two, Mr. Talbert."

"I'm aware of that, Miss Westerly."

"Well, bully for you," she said, folding her arms over her breasts. "Could we stick to the subject?"

"We *are* discussing the damn subject," he said, his voice rising as his hands curled into fists. "We're talking about being in love and making love a dozen years ago, and we're talking about making love . . . *making love*

. . . a few nights ago. Love *is* the subject, Minta, because I still love you, never stopped loving you, even when I thought you'd— But, dammit, who am I in love with? An eighteen-year-old girl, a memory? Or you, the woman you are now?"

He lunged to his feet and walked over to her, towering above her. She stared up at him, shock keeping her silent.

"Well, I want to know," he said, nearly yelling. "You're driving me crazy, lady, and I've had enough of this crap."

"*I'm* driving *you* crazy?" she shouted back. "I've got news for you, mister. I'm teetering on the edge of insanity because of you. I never stopped loving you, either, you big jerk, but the same question holds true. Who do I love? Nineteen-year-old Chism, my first love, my first lover? Or Chism Talbert, the man? If it's you, the man, then I've got lousy taste, because you're an extremely rude person. Quit screaming in my face, Talbert, or I'm going to punch you right in the nose."

Minta blinked. Oh, good night, she thought. What had she said? And Chism had said . . . Dear heaven.

Chism stiffened. What? Had he actually said that he . . . Had Minta really said that she . . .

"Well, isn't this . . . interesting," she said in a small voice. "My, my, we do have a little-bitty problem here, don't we?" A funny hiccupping sound escaped from her lips, followed by a sob.

"Oh, no," Chism said, his own voice now gentle. "Don't cry. Yell, punch me out, but please don't cry." He sat down beside her, slipping one arm around her shoulders. Lifting his free hand, he awkwardly patted her on the knee. "Everything will be fine, you'll see."

Minta made a fist and slugged him in the arm. "Don't patronize me."

"Ow! That hurt." He suddenly grinned. "Surely you've heard that it's better to make love than war."

"That," she said, with an indignant sniff, "was *not* funny."

His grin faded. "None of this is funny, Minta. It's a confusing mess. We have an important decision to make. We can close the book on what happened that summer and chalk up whatever we're feeling now as—as residual emotions."

"Residual emotions?" she repeated, then burst into laughter. She sobered with her next breath. "I'm sorry. I think I'm slightly hysterical. But residual emotions?"

He smiled. "I thought that sounded pretty good, considering that I'm winging it here."

"No comment. If that's Plan A, is there another choice, as in Plan B?"

Once more, his smile quickly vanished. "Yes, there's a Plan B. It deals with the present, with what's happening between us and discovering exactly what that is. I'm not sure how a person simply shuts off memories, but that's what we'd have to do. We've both said we want to know where our love is centered. Is it all based on old memories, or is it real, ours to have in the here and now?"

"This is all rather frightening, Chism. So much has taken place so quickly. I've spent too many years wondering what happened to us. I need to know what we're feeling now."

He nodded. "So do I. Plan B is in effect, then. You're not a eighteen-year-old girl, you're a woman. A beautiful woman." He lowered his head slowly toward hers. "You're a very sensuous, desirable woman. And I'm no longer a nineteen-year-old boy. I'm a man."

No joke, Minta thought giddily. And if he didn't kiss her, she was going to dissolve into a lifeless lump. His lips were so close, and she wanted him to . . . Well, there were just some things in this world that a woman had to do for herself.

She turned to him, encircled his neck with her arms, and kissed him for all she was worth.

He stiffened in surprise for an instant, then surrendered, returning her kiss with an intensity that seemed to steal the very breath from her body.

This, she mused dreamily, was most definitely a man, a magnificent, virile, exciting man. This was Chism Talbert. And as always whenever she was with him, the pulsing heat of desire swept through her, consuming her. She wanted him.

Remember Plan B, Arminta, a little voice taunted her. No memories of long ago were allowed to intrude into the present.

They weren't, she answered herself. This *was* now, and she was deeply, irrevocably in love with Chism Talbert.

A shiver coursed through her, and she trembled in his arms as he lifted his mouth from hers, only to string tantalizing kisses down her neck. When he reached the first button on her shirt, and his aching body urged him to go on, he raised his head. Staring at her lovely face, her eyes still closed, he knew he loved her. As a man, separate from the memories of the past, he loved her.

His eager libido protesting forcefully, he eased Minta away from him. She lifted her lashes to look at him questioningly, desire radiating clearly in her deep brown eyes.

"I think," he said hoarsely, "that we'd better slow down. That we want each other is a given. What we're not sure of is why." *He* was certain, but he had to give her time to discover her true feelings. Dear Lord, what if she didn't love him, except in her memories? No, he wouldn't dwell on that now. "Understand?"

"Yes," she whispered. She knew why she wanted to make love with him. She was *in* love with him. But she mustn't rush him. She could only wait, praying that what he felt for her was not made up of memories that would eventually fade and die. "We'll take this one step at a time."

He nodded and stood up, willing his body back under his control.

"I'd better leave," said Minta, getting to her feet as well. "I was baking earlier, and the kitchen is a mess. And, I have to stop for a few groceries, so I really must be on my way. It was clouding up a bit. I wonder—"

"Minta."

"—if we're going to have more rain. I brought in plenty of dry wood for the fire so—"

"Minta."

"No," she said, stepping back from him. "Don't say anything serious, anything that I'll have to find some place to put, because I don't have room for any more right now. Just let me chatter my way out the door, Chism."

He opened his mouth to speak, but said nothing. They gazed at each other for a long moment, then Minta spun around and nearly ran out of the house.

"You're mine," Chism said quietly to the empty room. "I love you, Minta." But, oh, God, what if she didn't love him?

As Minta drove away from Chism's house, she forced herself to concentrate only on what she needed from Lily Cushing's general store.

But what would it be like, she wondered, to cook dinner for Chism? No, better yet, they'd prepare the meal together, laughing, talking, sharing. After cleaning the kitchen, they'd settle in front of the fire and read, listen to music, perhaps watch an old movie on television.

Then, they'd climb the stairs and go to bed, together. Make love, together. Sleep, together, their heads resting on the same pillow as they snuggled through the night.

Oh, really? she thought dryly. And just where was she envisioning this romantic scenario taking place? At Willow Hill. Not in Manhattan, not in San Francisco, but in Haven Port, Maine.

Their children would know the joy of running barefoot through the grass, of picking wildflowers, of riding bicycles with the wind in their smiling faces, of having picnics beneath the old majestic willow tree. Their children would be Mainers, and all of them, as a family, would belong.

Sighing dejectedly, knowing full well her dreams might never come true, Minta stopped the car in front of the store. Smile, she told herself. Cheerfulness was the key word, as Lily Cushing was a dear, sweet, and *very* observant woman.

Minta entered the store with a bright, phony-feeling smile plastered on her face.

"Hello, hello," she said. "How are you today,

Mrs. . . ." She paused, realizing that Lily was nowhere in sight. "Hello?"

So much for that performance, Minta thought. Lily was probably in the rear storage area, or had gone upstairs to her living quarters for a moment.

Minta picked up one of the plastic baskets by the counter and turned to start toward the first aisle. A splash of color on the floor behind the counter caught her eye. Frowning, she set the basket down and leaned across the wide counter.

"Oh, dear heaven," she whispered. "Lily."

With her heart racing and a cold knot of fear tightening in her stomach, Minta ran behind the counter and dropped to her knees beside Lily. The older woman lay on the floor, her eyes closed and her face alarmingly pale. Minta cradled one of Lily's hands between hers, frightened at the feel of Lily's cold, clammy skin, but relieved when she found a pulse.

"Mrs. Cushing? Lily? Come on, you old sweetheart, open your eyes. Swooning went out about three generations ago. Lily? Oh, please, talk to me. I need a bottle of orange soda, Mrs. Cushing. What's this lying-down-on-the-job nonsense?" She gasped as fear clutched her. "Oh, God."

Leaping to her feet, she rushed to the telephone on the end of the counter. She hesitated, frantically searching her memory for the telephone number she hadn't used in a dozen years. After a moment, she snatched up the receiver and dialed.

One ring . . . two . . .

"Hello?" a deep voice said.

"Chism? Oh, thank heavens."

"Minta? What is it? What's wrong?"

"Chism, it's Mrs. Cushing. I found her on the floor here at the store. She's unconscious, doesn't respond to my voice or—"

"I'm on my way."

"Thank you," she said to the dial tone, then replaced the receiver.

She returned to Lily's side and grasped her hand again. For what seemed like an eternity, she spoke to Lily, urging her to wake up, telling her that the floor was no place for an afternoon nap, begging her to open her eyes and smile, to tend to the store as she always had.

At last Minta heard the squeal of tires outside. Moments later, Chism burst through the door and ran around the counter.

"Oh, Chism," Minta whispered, "she hasn't moved."

He dropped to one knee and placed his fingertips on the side of Lily's neck. "Her pulse is weak."

"What do you think is wrong?"

"I don't know. Heart attack, maybe, or a stroke. I called the doctor, but his wife said he's making a few house calls. She's trying to reach him, but it may take too long. The nearest hospital is in Portland, and the best thing to do is to drive her there ourselves. Go upstairs and get a blanket and pillow."

"All right."

Minta ran to the rear of the store where stairs led to the upper level. When she returned, no further words were exchanged as she and Chism set about their task. Lily was short but plump, and Chism struggled as he lifted her.

Minta opened the door for him, then hurried to her car, helping him lay Lily on the backseat. Minta sat on the floor next to her, as Chism slid behind the wheel.

"You're going to be fine, just fine," Minta told the unconscious woman as Chism sped toward Portland. "Haven Port just wouldn't be Haven Port without you running the general store. We need you there, we really do."

"Minta," Chism said as he whipped past a car, "I don't think she can hear you."

Minta sighed. "I know. Lord, I hate this, Chism. She's such a wonderful person, so caring and warm. Does she have family? I realize she's been a widow for years, and she doesn't have any children. But what about other relatives?"

"No, there's no one. Her life is that store. Her family is the people of Haven Port. She's been there for as long as I can remember. Bottom line, though, is that she's alone."

"No, she's not," Minta said fiercely. "She's

not alone, Chism. We're here. Lily, just hang on. Chism and I are with you. We'll be here for you, Lily, together. Right, Chism?"

Chism's hands tightened on the steering wheel. "Right. You and I . . . together."

Willow Hill
September 26, 1892

Dear Diary,
  Time.
  It seems to be slipping through my fingers like grains of sand, despite my efforts to hold fast to it, keep it still.
  Time has become my enemy, as it marches on like a hungry beast, devouring the hours and days that remain before we are scheduled to return to New York.
  Papa took the train down to New York to assess the decorating of our house, and returned yesterday to report that all is well and proceeding as planned.
  Our time here in Haven Port grows short.
  I told my beloved Joseph what Papa had said. Joseph took my hand in his, looked

directly into my eyes, and said, "Marry me, Arminta. We'll leave here, create a whole new life just for the two of us. Please, Arminta, say you'll become my wife."

Oh, dearest diary, how can I express the joy I felt, the sensation of my heart nearly bursting with love?

I smiled at him and said the one word that will change the entire course of my life.

"Yes."

I do not wish to hurt Mama and Papa, to cause them pain or disappointment, but there is no way to keep that from happening. I shall marry Joseph, be his wife, bear his children. I have made my choice, and my heart sings with joy as I envision a future with him.

Yet if only I could stop time and grant Joseph and me the hours we need to make our plans. Time remains the foe, however, and we must persevere in spite of its unrelenting and rapid pace.

Soon, I hope, time will cease to be the enemy and become the glorious years stretching before us as Joseph and I share the future . . . together.

But now, dearest diary, time demands that I sleep.

Good night.

Sincerely,

Arminta Masterson

Eight

Willow Hill
September 15, 1990

Time.

So much time had passed, Minta thought, since the nurses had taken Lily through the gray double doors of the emergency room. Time seemed to have become a thing with nearly human qualities, hovering in that horrible waiting area like a dreaded enemy.

"Chism," she said, "what's taking so long?"

"It's only been twenty minutes, Minta." He patted the cushion next to him on the brown cracked leather sofa. "Why don't you come sit down? You're not going to accomplish anything by wearing out the tile on the floor."

She sighed and sank down next to him.

"Do you want some coffee?" he asked.

"No, thank you. I don't want anything but to hear that Lily is going to be all right."

He turned to look at her, a frown knitting his brows together. "You really care deeply about Lily, don't you?" he said.

"Yes, I do. She's been a part of my life since I was a child. You seemed surprised that I'm upset."

"I guess I am. I mean, she's a great lady, but she's a Mainer. You were always one of the summer people and—"

"Dammit, Chism! Would you quit labeling me like I'm some kind of social disease? I'm a person, a human being, and so is Lily. You say you're tired of the class distinction, but you certainly sound like your father's son."

Anger flashed in Chism's eyes, then disappeared in the next instant.

"You're right," he said. "I stand guilty as charged, and I apologize."

"Apology accepted," Minta said, her voice gentling. "We're just two people who are very worried about our friend. That's what's important. Lily and what's happening behind those doors." She paused. "Oh, Lord, what is taking so long?"

Chism grasped one of Minta's hands and placed it on his thigh. "Hey, take it easy. I've never seen you so upset. But then, I guess we've never been in a situation like this one. When my dad was sick, I had to develop a lot of patience, the old hurry-up-and-wait routine. The difference now is that . . . well, we're not alone."

"No, we're not alone," Minta said softly, staring into his eyes. "When I found Lily, calling you was automatic. I needed you and . . ."

"I came. I came for Lily, yes, but, Minta, if you needed me, I'd come no matter how far away you were, or what the problem was."

"I know. I'm not even certain why I'm so positive of that, but I realize that what you're saying is true." And it added yet another layer to the depth of her love for him. "Thank you, Chism."

"That's just part of being . . . being good friends," he said.

Please, Minta, he thought, say it's more than that. What they could have together went far beyond friendship. What would she say if he just opened his mouth and told her how he felt? No, not yet, not now. He had to protect himself as he watched for clues that she loved him in kind.

"Good friends," she repeated, attempting a smile that failed. "Yes, well, during that last summer, I considered you my best friend because I knew I could tell you everything. I could count on you to always be there for me, and I came to understand that the person you love must also be your best friend."

"We're not dwelling on that summer, remember?"

"Yes, but it *did* happen, Chism. Who we are

today is the sum total of all that's gone before."

He released her hand and got to his feet. "That's a textbook theory." He turned to look down at her. "Minta, we have to concentrate on the present. We could make a terrible mistake if we confused old emotions with new ones."

"I understand that, but—"

"Excuse me," a voice said.

Chism spun around as Minta jumped to her feet. An older man wearing a white coat had entered the room.

"I'm Dr. Hill," he said. "You're the couple who brought in Lily Cushing, aren't you?"

"Yes," Chism said. "Lily doesn't have any family. We're . . . well, we're her family. This is Minta Westerly, and I'm Chism Talbert."

"Nice to meet you," Dr. Hill said.

"How's Lily?" Minta asked. "What's wrong with her?"

"She's a lucky woman," the doctor said. "She's had a mild heart attack that didn't cause any real damage. It was her body's way of warning her that she was getting into trouble. Her blood pressure is high, she's overweight, she's working too hard. She's got to slow down, shed some pounds, stay on a low-fat and low-cholesterol diet."

"Oh, boy," Chism said, shaking his head. "Lily loves to bake, and she enjoys eating what she makes. She also runs a general store like a marine sergeant. She does everything herself and is one independent woman."

Dr. Hill chuckled. "Believe me, she made that clear during the conversation I just had with her. I'm going to keep her here for a few days to get her blood pressure under control and have a nutritionist map out a diet for her. She's already ranting and raving because no one is tending the store."

"May we see her?" Minta asked.

"For a few minutes. Don't stay long, though. Her system has had a shock, and she needs to rest. She's been taken up to room four-fifteen. If you leave a number where I can reach you, I'll let you know when she can go home."

"Thank you," Chism said.

"I just hope she realizes," the doctor went on, "that she's got to make some major changes in her life. She's a stubborn woman, that's for sure. You two pop in for a quick hello, then be on your way."

"We will," Minta said. "Thank you for everything."

Lily Cushing was *not* smiling when Minta and Chism entered her room.

"There you are!" she exclaimed. "Get my clothes and take me home."

"Whoa," Chism said. "You're not going anywhere for a few days, Lily Cushing. We have all the facts. You're on a diet as of now, and you're not going to be working so hard in that store."

"Pshaw," said Lily, glaring at him. "I should be at the store right this minute. You tell me, Chism Talbert, what the folks of Haven Port are going to do without Lily Cushing's general store. I'm needed there, got no business lying in bed being badgered by an old coot who says I'm too fat. Now, find my clothes. I've got work to do, a store to run, bread to bake."

"You're not moving," Minta said, "and—*I'm* running the store."

"What?" Chism and Lily said in unison.

"Well, why not?" Minta said. "I have plenty of free time, and heaven knows it won't be as stressful as my job in Manhattan. *My* doctor couldn't possibly object to the idea. It's perfect. The store will stay open, I'll enjoy it, and you'll rest easy, Lily, knowing that the people of Haven Port have access to what they need."

Lily tapped one pudgy finger against her chin. "Has possibilities." Then she shook her head. "No, it won't do. I'm as strong as an ox, but you'd be blown away by a New England breeze, Minta Westerly. Those cartons of canned goods are heavy to tote out from the back room to stock the shelves." She slid a glance at Chism, then sighed dramatically. "Best just find my clothes and take my decrepit body back to Haven Port so I can tend to business."

Chism crossed his arms over his chest and

cocked one eyebrow. "And if I say I'll help Minta in the store?" he asked. "You know, tote the boxes, help stock the shelves, carry out heavy parcels for the ladies. What then?"

Lily beamed. "Why, I'd just lie here as contented as a sow in a mud patch, following every silly order that pompous old doctor gave me. Ayuh, knowing you and Minta were tending my store together would surely ease my mind."

Chism chuckled and shook his head. "You're a con artist, Lily Cushing, but you win. Minta and I will run the store."

"Good," Lily said. "Now, shoo. I'm tired."

Minta kissed Lily's cheek. "We'll see you soon. Behave yourself."

"Thank you both for . . . well, for everything. You're dear to my heart, both of you."

Minta and Chism smiled at her, then left the room.

"Together," Lily said to no one. "The way it was meant to be." She closed her eyes, a smile lingering on her lips.

After leaving Portland, Chism announced that he was hungry, and Minta voiced no objection to stopping at a restaurant he chose that was casual and homey, decorated in a nautical theme. Even the waiters and waitresses were dressed in old-fashioned sailor suits.

Sea gulls made out of cloth, papier-mâché, plaster, iron, and a multitude of other mediums, perched on every bit of spare space.

After the waitress had taken their order for seafood platters, Chism glanced around and chuckled.

"They're really into sea gulls," he said.

"I think it's a charming place," Minta said. "Very quaint." She paused. "Do you realize that this is the first time we've ever gone out to dinner together? We had picnics that summer, but we didn't go to a café or restaurant. Oh, well, it's not important."

"Yes, it is," he said. "Going out to dinner is a normal occurrence in a relationship."

She laughed. "Are you saying that what we did that summer wasn't normal?"

"I'm serious, Minta. And, no, it wasn't normal. We were young and we loved the daring of it, the excitement of sneaking around, making certain we weren't discovered. This"—he gestured to the room—"is real, the way it should be." He met her gaze. "I'm glad you're here."

"So am I," she said softly.

Time, which had been the enemy while they waited for word on Lily, now lost meaning. The restaurant and its sea gulls faded into a mist, leaving only Minta and Chism, and the passion that swirled within them. It was as though they were encased in a sensual cocoon that kept the rest of the world at bay.

Silently, they each declared their love, but no words were spoken as they stayed behind their protective walls. But the desire gleamed in their eyes, caused their hearts to race, the blood to pound hot and quick in their veins. Memories of their lovemaking captured them, and their passion flared like a brightly burning flame.

"Lord, Minta," Chism muttered at last.

"I know." she whispered. "I feel it too. Oh, Chism, I want—"

"Here's your salads," their waitress said cheerfully.

Minta jumped in surprise, then moved back to make room for the plate. She stared down at the salad as though she'd never seen one before in her life.

"Eat," Chism said gruffly as he picked up his fork.

"Right."

A few minutes later the waitress returned with their dinners, and Minta and Chism continued to eat in silence.

"Why did you offer to run Lily's store?" Chism asked finally.

"Because I knew she'd be all in a dither if it stayed closed. She has to be calm and relaxed so the doctors can help her. Besides, it'll be fun. I'm actually looking forward to working there. It'll give me a chance to get to know more of the townfolk better too."

"Why would you want to?"

"Because I've definitely decided to quit my job and stay on in Haven Port." What? Minta asked herself. When had she reached *that* momentous decision? She really didn't know, but she was certain the decision was right. She was going to live in Haven Port, Maine, and, finally, really belong. "Why are you frowning, Chism?"

"Have you thought this through? The life-style here, especially in the winter, is so different from Manhattan. Don't you think you're being just a bit hasty?"

"No."

"You'll be bored out of your mind."

"No."

"The Mainers will seem dull compared to the yuppie set you're used to."

"No."

"What about your career?"

"I'll do free-lance work."

"You have an answer for everything, don't you?" he said, still glowering.

"No, I don't," she said quietly. "There are still a great many questions without answers." Such as what was going to happen to them? "Many, many questions."

Chism stared at her for a long moment, then forced himself to eat more of the food he no longer wanted.

Minta was actually going to do it, he thought incredulously. She was going to move to Haven Port and live at Willow Hill. It was crazy. As soon as the snow started flying—in October—she'd develop such a severe case of culture shock, she'd hightail it right back to the city.

And where did he fit into this new scenario of hers? he wondered. She knew he lived in San Francisco and was only in Haven Port temporarily. Of course, it was obvious to anyone bothering to notice that he wasn't exactly rushing to leave Maine. Was she envisioning a future with him at Willow Hill? Or did she see herself bidding him adieu and getting on with her new life? Oh, yes, there certainly were a lot of questions.

And they were questions he hadn't yet mustered the courage to ask.

He gave up attempting to choke down any more food and pushed his plate aside.

"This is where we do the chitchat, getting-to-know-you-better bit," he said, watching Minta eat. "The thing is, Minta, I already know a lot of interesting little details about you."

"Oh?" she mumbled as she took a bite of flaky fish.

"Yep. I know that your favorite color is pink, which is the color of the candle you used to signal me that you were coming to meet me. I know that when you were in the seventh grade, you wrote a book report on *Gone with the Wind* and changed the ending. Rhett *did* give a damn, and he and Scarlett lived happily ever after, along with their six kids. The teacher gave you a failing grade."

Minta set her fork down with a shaking hand. "Chism . . ."

"I know," he went on, his voice low as he pinned her in place with his dark gaze, "that you like peas, but hate green beans. You're scared to death of fuzzy caterpillars, but you think ladybugs are cute. You eat the frosting first, then the cake, and go barefoot whenever possible because you detest shoes."

"Chism, don't. Why are you doing this? You learned all those things that last summer. They're part of the memories. We're supposed to be dealing with the present."

"I realize that, but I can't erase the entire past, or the fact that I *do* know a multitude of special, personal things about you. Very special, very personal things."

A warm flush crept onto her cheeks. "That's enough. I don't know what you're trying to prove by this trip down memory lane, but I don't want to hear any more."

He leaned back in his chair and stared out the window at the gathering darkness. He didn't know what he was trying to prove, either. He'd suddenly been consumed by a wave of anger, though, and a refusal to dismiss the memories of that summer as though none of it had actually happened.

Granted, the plan to discover who Minta and he were now was sound. But, dammit, they weren't strangers. He knew Arminta Masterson Westerly. And he loved her.

He wanted to spend the rest of his life with her. In Haven Port, Maine? Fine. He could run his business from anywhere that he chose.

But what he still didn't know was how Minta felt about him. Plus, there was her newsflash that she was giving up her entire life in Manhattan to move to Willow Hill. What had started as a niggling doubt that she'd really be content in Haven Port was steadily growing into a strong suspicion that she'd never be happy there. New York, with its glitz and glamour, would beckon, and she'd leave him. Again.

"Have you finished eating," he asked abruptly, "or do you want dessert?"

"I can live without dessert," she said, "and without your suddenly less-than-sunshine mood." She casually examined her pale pink nail polish. "I certainly hope you're not grumpy tomorrow morning, Mr. Talbert. I really must insist that my employee at the general store be of a pleasant nature. It's important from a public-relations standpoint, you see."

He flattened his hands on the table and leaned toward her. "*Your* employee?"

"Well, yes. I, after all, was the one who volunteered to run Lily's store. You offered to help me. I, therefore, am in charge."

"Bull," he said, glaring at her. He signaled to the waitress for the bill. "We're in this together, Minta, equal partners." He pushed back his chair and stood. "Together. Understand?"

"Together," she repeated, smiling sweetly. She stood, then patted him on the cheek. "That is certainly becoming an interesting word. I'll wait for you outside."

Chism narrowed his eyes as he watched Minta walk away with a rather exaggerated sway to her hips. Then, of its own volition, a smile crept onto his lips and grew into a grin. He shook his head and chuckled.

She was really something, he thought. And he needed her. She would warm the chill of loneliness within him, fill the void in his life, make him complete. They would have everything, and more, that they had shared that enchanted summer long ago.

Somehow, he vowed, he had to keep Minta by his side for the remainder of his days.

"There you go, Mrs. Riley," Minta said. Chism, thank heavens, had been quick to introduce her to everyone who had come into the store during the past two days. "Can you manage that sack, or would you like Chism to carry it out for you?"

The elderly woman laughed. "He'd have to accompany me all the way home, dear. This is my day for walking. I've come from the other side of the inlet at a brisk, peppy pace."

"That's quite a trek," said Minta, smiling.

"Ayuh, and you can be assured that Lily Cushing is going to get in plenty of miles with me when she gets home. There's time to walk many a day before the weather goes to bad. I'll be giving her the very Jesse if she puts up a fuss. The doctor wants her to lose weight, so I'll get her walking. Well, I'm off." She turned to go, then looked back, "Westerly. Minta Westerly. Are you that little sprite who had the shiny bright yellow bike years ago?"

"I am, indeed."

"You're summer people. Willow Hill, isn't it? Yes, Willow Hill. Well, isn't that fine that you'd see fit to take care of Lily's store while she's poorly. Oh, my, I do remember that pretty bicycle."

"She painted it purple," said Chism, coming up to the counter.

"Oh, that's right," Mrs. Riley said. "I recall that now. Never did decide if I liked it better yellow or purple."

"Yellow," Chism said.

"Purple," Minta said.

Mrs. Riley laughed. "Squabble it out between you." She peered at Minta. "Did you forget to leave on Labor Day, dear?"

"No, ma'am," she said, smiling. "I'm staying on permanently at Willow Hill."

"Is that a fact? That's splendid, truly lovely news. It does an old heart good to see young faces among us. And our Chism is back too.

This is happy tidings to be spread. Welcome, Minta Westerly."

"Thank you, Mrs. Riley," she said softly. "Thank you very much."

The bell over the door tinkled as Mrs. Riley bustled out, then a heavy silence fell. Minta fiddled with some pencils that stood in a mug on the counter while she struggled to bring her emotions under control.

Chism walked around the counter and handed her a folded white cotton handkerchief. She took it without meeting his gaze and dabbed at her eyes.

"Not all Mainers," he said quietly, "think like my father did. Mrs. Riley has accepted you, and the majority of the others will too. You'll belong, Minta, if you stay here. You'll belong, just like you've always wanted to. I can't begin to tell you how sorry I am for my father's attitude, for what he did to you, to us."

"It's not your fault," she said. "Your father loved you, and was trying to keep you from being hurt." She took a steadying breath, then looked up at him. "Enough of my waterworks. It's just that Mrs. Riley was so sweet. She made me feel very special."

Chism drew a thumb over her cheek, catching a lingering tear. "You *are* special," he said huskily. "I've watched you the past two days, Minta. You have a way of making everyone who comes in here feel as though he or she is the most important person to ever walk through that door. Lily does that too. It's a gift, the way you relate to people. I admire and respect that."

"Thank you, Chism. You have a lot of patience with people yourself. You appeared totally captivated when Mrs. McNeil was telling you her recipe for prune-nut muffins. I guess we're seeing a part of each other that we didn't know was there. We didn't have a chance to interact with people during that last summer."

"I don't think I would have shared you with anyone anyway."

She smiled. "We didn't see, or think, beyond the moment we were living." Be careful, Minta, she admonished herself. She mustn't slip back in time. "Well, the hour is here to lock up and go home for today."

"Have you told your parents about your plans to stay on?"

"Yes, I called them last night. My mother said it sounded like a marvelous idea. She suggested I sublet my apartment in Manhattan so it would be there in case I decided I wasn't cut out for the quiet life here."

"I see," he said, his jaw tightening slightly. "Have you informed your boss about your plans?"

"Yes, I called him too." She laughed. "He yelled and screamed, but he yells and screams about everything. He's a very nice man. He just became a grandfather, and everyone keeps out of his way because he always has a fistful of new pictures of the baby. He said I'd come back to work there once I realized I was stagnating here. He made it very clear that there'd always be a place waiting for me at the firm."

"Well, you certainly have all your bets covered, don't you?" Chism said, a hard edge to his voice.

Minta frowned. "What do you mean?"

"You have a safety clause to your radical idea to move here." He dragged a restless hand through his hair. "At the first hint of cabin fever this winter, you can chuck it all and go running back to the big city. How very convenient."

She planted her hands on her hips. "What are you so angry about all of a sudden? I'm just answering your questions about who I've told about my plans."

"And I'm listening, hearing loud and clear that you won't have burned any bridges. You won't be taking any risks by moving to Willow Hill."

"You're yelling at me because my boss thinks enough of me to let me know I'll always be welcome there? Well, excuse me all to hell for being competent, excellent actually, in the field of advertising. Lord, you're moody. You're grumpy too. It's a good thing you work with computers, Chism. They don't care if you're pleasant or not."

"Hey, I listened to every detail of that prune-nut muffin recipe, didn't I? I'm just afraid Mrs. McNeil is going to bake me some of those awful things."

Minta opened her mouth to retort, then closed it and shook her head. "What are we arguing about? We were talking, then . . . Did I miss something?"

Chism stared up at the ceiling for a moment, then met her gaze.

"I'm sorry," he said. "It's my fault. I'm edgy, but that's no excuse to jump all over you."

"Are you . . . are you eager to get back to San Francisco?" she asked. Did he want to leave her? "I'm sure you have a lot to do there. As soon as Lily gets home, I'm going to New York to take care of everything that needs doing so I can move here. You'll be free to go then, too, Chism. In fact, I could handle things here for the next couple of days, if you'd prefer to be on your way."

This was it, she thought. Truth time.

"Is that what you want me to do?" he said quietly. He knew he was stripping himself bare, making himself vulnerable as hell. But he had to know. He couldn't put it off any longer. "Minta?"

She swallowed hard, then lifted her chin as she looked directly into his eyes.

"No," she said. "I don't want you to leave. I love you, Chism Talbert. I loved you when I was eighteen, and I love you now. I loved you as a child. I love you as a woman. There it is, the truth. Please don't feel guilty if you can't return my love. I'll understand. I'll be fine and—"

"Shut up."

"Well, you don't have to be rude."

He reached out, hauled her to him, and covered her mouth with his in a searing, breath-stealing kiss. Finally, he raised his head and spoke, his lips still on hers.

"I don't want to go back to my life in San Francisco. I don't want to leave you, ever. I love you, Arminta Masterson Westerly. I loved you as a boy, and I love you now, as a man."

"Oh, Chism," she said, throwing her arms around him. "My Chism."

"Let's go home."

She smiled giddily. "Your place or mine?"

"We'll go to Willow Hill for now, but it's your parents' house. We'll build our own that will be filled with *our* memories. What I'm saying, Minta, is that I want to marry you, raise our children in Haven Port, spend the rest of our lives together. Will you? Marry me?"

"Oh, yes. Yes, my love. Oh, Chism, I'm so happy."

They left the store, and were met by a chill wind. Chism shivered, but he knew it had nothing to do with the dropping temperature.

He should be grinning from ear to ear, he told himself. The woman he loved had just agreed to marry him. The woman he loved returned his love. But the knot of fear in his gut just wouldn't go away.

How long would Minta be content in Haven Port?

Willow Hill
September 23, 1892

Dear Diary,
   Happiness.
   I have never known such happiness. The word itself seems to dance through the air like a carefree elf as I allow it to escape from my lips.
   Oh, where to begin to tell you what has transpired? My beloved Joseph has spoken with Papa, and has asked for my hand in marriage.
   I had no hint that Joseph planned to do such a daring deed as this, but when Papa was in the carriage house, Joseph approached him. Papa was shocked, of course, but he listened to everything Joseph had to say.

I suspected nothing when Papa requested my presence in the library. Mama was there, and I saw immediately that she was distressed. She was pale, and her eyes were puffy, as if she'd been crying.

When Papa told me what Joseph had done, I sank onto a chair, my legs trembling so badly I could no longer stand without support.

"And you, Arminta?" Papa asked me. "How do you feel about this young man?"

My voice was quivering like a scared child's when I spoke.

"I love Joseph, Papa," I said. "He is my life, my love. I wish to spend the remainder of my days by his side as his wife."

"My darling child," Mama said, "he has so little to offer you."

"No, Mama, he has everything to offer me. His love. He has brought sunshine into my life, a happiness I have never known."

"And if we refuse to give you our blessings?" Papa asked.

Dizziness swept over me, but I gathered my courage.

"I have no wish to cause you pain," I said, "but you must understand that I am a woman grown, who knows her own mind. Forced to choose, I would stay with Joseph. That is how it should be when two people love each other. Please don't cause me to start my life with Joseph with the dark cloud of your rejection hovering over us. He loves me, he truly does."

"I know," Papa said. "There is no doubt in my mind about his feelings for you. He is proud, Arminta, and is determined to care for you without the resources I could provide. You shall not possess what has always been at your fingertips if you marry him."

"I realize that," I said. "Oh, Mama, Papa, please, can't you understand what I have with Joseph? How much I love him? The happiness that touches my very soul?"

The silence in the room at my words was oppressive, like a crushing weight.

Then Mama spoke. "Yes, Arminta, I understand. You feel for Joseph what I do for your father. You shall marry the man of your heart, my darling child, and I wish you a lifetime of joy together."

"So be it," Papa said. "Let the tongues wag and the gossip flow. All that is important is your happiness, Arminta. You have our blessings."

Oh, dearest diary, I seem to be floating above the ground, my feet not quite touching the earth beneath me. Happiness flows within me like the peach brandy I sip at Christmastime.

When I told Joseph of my parents' decision, he lifted me into his arms and swung me around, the smile on his face one of the most beautiful sights I have ever seen.

Then we went to sit by the willow tree to make our plans for the future. A future together. A future of happiness.

Soon, very soon, I shall marry my beloved. I shall be Mrs. Joseph Westerly for all time.

Good night.

Sincerely,

Arminta Masterson

Nine

Willow Hill
September 19, 1990

Happiness.

In the foggy state of just awakening, Minta whispered the word. Dawn's light was growing stronger, announcing the arrival of the new day, but she delayed leaving the warmth of her bed.

Happiness, she thought, turning her head to gaze at Chism, who slept beside her. How magnificent he was, even asleep, the power of his body still evident. She loved him beyond words.

Happiness, she supposed, was a subjective term, having a different meaning to each person. She'd often seen greeting cards with cute pictures and sayings like, "Happiness is a new puppy," "Happiness is a Rolls-Royce," "Happiness is a dill pickle."

But to her, happiness was Chism Talbert.

Their lovemaking the night before had been exquisite. Their intimacy had sealed their commitment, a mutual giving and taking of their deep love. The future lay before them like a brilliant path, beckoning to them to move forward and reap its multitude of rewards.

Oh, Chism, she thought. They had waited so many years for what they now had together. Life had brought them full circle, back to Haven Port and Willow Hill, back to each other. Life was so strange, and so wonderful. And happiness held center stage with Chism.

He slowly opened his eyes. "Hi."

"Hi," she said, smiling. "I love you."

He slid his hand beneath the sheet to gently cup one of her breasts. "I love you too. You're nice to wake up to. I used to fantasize about what it would be like to spend the night with you, to see you, touch you, make love to you in the early morning."

"Well, you've spent the night, you've seen me, you're touching me, so . . ."

"We computer whizzes are very detail-oriented," he said. "I have one more thing on that list to take care of."

"I'm a firm believer in making a list, then seeing that everything on it is accomplished."

"Good."

He swept her up to lie on top of him, wove

his fingers through her hair, and brought her mouth down to his.

The world beyond the sunny bedroom was forgotten.

"Oh, it's grand to be home," Lily said as she entered the store. "That hospital was a dreary place. Thank you for coming for me, Chism."

"My pleasure, ma'am."

"And my thanks to you both," she went on, smiling at Minta, "for tending the store while I was away. Everything looks wonderful, absolutely perfect."

Minta came from behind the counter and gave Lily a hug. "We enjoyed every minute," she said. "Now, I think you should go upstairs and rest for a bit."

"Mercy, no," Lily said. "All I've done for days is lie on my backside, which that obnoxious doctor has informed me is too broad."

"You've got to take things easier around here," Chism said. "There are plenty of boys who would be glad to have an after-school job stocking shelves."

Lily wrinkled her nose. "I don't now that I'd like a young boy fiddling with my stock."

Chism folded his arms over his chest. "Lily Cushing, you have no choice. You're going to hire help here, you're going on a diet, and you're trekking around the inlet with Mrs. Riley three times a week. You're going to take good care of yourself, even if I have to check up on you like a warden."

Glaring at him, Lily started to retort, but he forestalled her.

"After all," he added, exchanging a quick smile with Minta, "somewhere down the road Minta and I will need a baby-sitter. A person has to be in tip-top shape to handle a busy baby."

"Baby?" Lily said, staring at both of them. "You're going to need a baby-sitter?"

"Well, not right away," Minta said, laughing. "We're not trying to break it to you gently that I'm pregnant, because I'm not. What we are saying is that Chism and I plan to be married and live in Haven Port. We'll be staying at Willow Hill until we can buy some land and build our own home."

"Oh," Lily said, whipping a hankie from her pocket. "That's wonderful. I'm so happy for you both." She blew her nose. "Dear me, I'd best lose some pounds if I'm to trundle after a toddler in the future. Walking with Sarah Riley will be on my calendar. And I'll post a sign on the door saying I'm looking for part-time after-school help."

"Excellent," Minta said.

Lily sighed. "A wedding. I adore weddings. When is it to be?"

"Soon," Minta said. "We called my parents this morning and told them the news. They're delighted. Chism and I have loose ends to tie up in Manhattan and San Francisco. Once that's done, we can concentrate on setting a date for the wedding."

"Oh, Chism," Lily said, "I do so wish your father was here to witness all of this. He'd be so pleased, so happy for you."

Chism's jaw tightened slightly. "Yeah, well . . ."

"No, no gloomy thoughts," Lily said. "Goodness, I can hardly wait to spread the news. Let me see, who should I call first?"

As Lily chattered on, Minta and Chism smiled at each other, love shining in their eyes.

That evening, Minta and Chism sat close together on the sofa in front of the fireplace, watching the leaping flames.

Minta leaned her head on Chism's shoulder. "I'm so contented, like a sleepy kitten."

He kissed the top of her head. "Good."

"Chism, I think it would be best if I go to New York early tomorrow morning. The sooner I go, the quicker I'll be able to tend to everything and get back here where I really belong."

He frowned slightly. "I suppose you're right. I could go to San Francisco tomorrow if I can get a flight out. There's no sense in being separated longer than we have to. We'll go at the same time."

"That's a marvelous idea."

"It's settled then. As they say in the movies, 'We'll meet back at the pass.' That's Willow Hill, in case you're wondering."

She laughed softly. "Got it."

Early the next morning, Chism stood in the driveway of Willow Hill and lifted one hand in a last wave as Minta drove away. The car disappeared from view, and he shoved his hands into the back pockets of his jeans and continued to stare down the empty road.

The familiar knot tightened in his stomach, and a chilling sense of foreboding dropped over him like a heavy shroud. He wanted to jump in his father's rickety truck and chase after Minta, not allow her out of his sight as she was swallowed up in the sea of people and the surge of activity in New York.

He wanted to tell her over and over again how much he loved her, what a wonderful future they would have together. She knew that, though. Dammit, he thought, why didn't he trust her more? Of course she had to settle her affairs in Manhattan before she could settle in Haven Port. He knew that what had happened at the end of that long-ago summer had not been her fault. She hadn't left him willingly.

Yet the fear within him refused to dissipate, and he remained standing in front of the house, staring down the empty road.

Minta glanced around her office one last time, making certain she'd packed all the personal items into the cardboard box.

She would miss the people here, she mused, but *not* the never-ending stress and pressure. It had been a challenging career, and she was extremely proud of her accomplishments. Still, she knew without a doubt that it was time for a change, a new era in her life.

And she would share it with Chism.

"So, Minta," a voice said, jolting her back to the present, "you're all packed and ready to desert this crazy ship."

She smiled at the portly man who'd entered her office. "I certainly am, boss. It's been wonderful working here, Henry, but I know that what I'm doing is right for me."

"If you say so. Hey, did I show you the latest pictures of my grandson? Oh, yes, I did. I suppose you'll be bouncing a baby on your knee one of these days."

"I hope so. Haven Port will be a marvelous place for Chism and me to raise our children."

"You're changing your entire lifestyle."

"I most definitely am. I'll still have my hand in advertising, *if* I can line up some free-lance work."

"So you said. I think I can help you with that. There's a small radio station upstate that wants to project a new image. They need a package for newspaper ads, flyers, hype spots during their broadcasts. It's not big enough for me to assign a team to it, but you could handle it on your own."

"It sounds perfect."

"Why don't I give them a call and suggest they hire you? It'll be my going-away present to you. Can I tell the owner you'd be willing to come up and see him with a package proposal in a few days? I have his budget figures on my desk."

"Well," Minta said slowly, "I wanted to get back to Willow Hill as quickly as possible . . ." She paused. "No, this is a wonderful opportunity to launch my free-lance business. I'd be foolish to pass it up. Chism will understand if I'm delayed. I've already sublet my apartment and shipped my personal items to Willow Hill, but I can stay at my parents' while I'm preparing the presentation. Thank you, Henry, this is really very kind of you."

"Just remember that you're always welcome to come back to work here." He chuckled. "You're the only one who still gushes over the pictures of my grandson."

She walked around the desk and kissed him on the cheek. "You're a sweetheart. I'll drop in from time to time to say hello when Chism and I come into the city."

"Be happy, Minta."

"Guaranteed. Chism and I are going to have a wonderful life together."

"Are you certain he'll understand why you're delaying your return to Maine?"

"Oh, I'm sure he will. He's in business for himself too. He'll realize how important this is to getting my free-lance career off the ground. Oh, yes, Chism will be pleased for me."

Chism's grip on the telephone tightened until his knuckles turned white.

"So, there you have it," Minta was saying. "Isn't it exciting? Henry was such a dear to do this for me."

"Yeah, it's great."

"I'm going to put in long hours preparing the package for the radio station, so I can present it to them as soon as possible. Is everything all right at Willow Hill?"

No! he thought. Minta wasn't there, with him, where she belonged. How in the hell could she think that everything was all right?

"Chism?"

"It's getting colder," he said. "Since I came back from San Francisco yesterday, I've had a fire going almost continually."

"Marvelous. I can hardly wait to get back there. I miss you so much, Chism."

Oh, really? he thought dryly. She missed him, but not enough to delay starting her free-lance business. The radio-station deal had been dangled in front of her nose, and she'd grabbed it and run. What he'd been afraid of was happening already.

"I miss you too," he said, rubbing one hand over the back of his neck. "You didn't have to start your new endeavor now, Minta. I have plenty of money. There are several parcels of land for sale around here that we should look at. They won't be on the market long."

"Oh. Well, I trust your judgment, Chism. If you find one that will suit our needs, put a deposit on it. I'm sure I'll like whatever you pick."

"You don't have any idea when you'll be back?"

"Not yet. It will be as soon as possible, believe me. I love you, Chism. I'll call again tomorrow night. Okay?"

"Yeah, sure," he said. "I love you, Minta. I want you here with me."

"And I want to be there. Soon, my love. 'Bye for now."

"Good night," he said, and slowly replaced the receiver.

His glance skimmed over the room, coming to rest on the family photographs on the mantel. He felt like an intruder here, he thought suddenly. There he stood in Willow Hill, acting as though it were his own. When Minta had been there, it hadn't bothered him.

But Minta *wasn't* there now, and she had no idea when she would be. Yes, she was launching her new business, but couldn't she have put it on hold for a while and concentrated on them? The lure of Manhattan, the challenge and excitement of her career, had already won out over the love she had for him.

Once again he was the Mainer and she was one of the summer people.

He, and what he had to offer, didn't measure up.

Minta Westerly had a shiny yellow bike, and Chism Talbert had nothing.

He surged to his feet as a restlessness gripped him, urging him to move, to do something physical, before he exploded from pent-up emotions. He strode across the room, snatched his jacket from the hall closet, and stalked out into the cold, dark night.

The fire continued to burn in the hearth, offering warmth and a soft, welcoming glow. But there was no one at Willow Hill to receive it.

In the late afternoon of the last day of September, Minta turned into the driveway at Willow Hill.

Memories.

She shut off the ignition, then she sat perfectly still for a moment, allowing the memories to float over her. Willow Hill held so many of those memories, and the most precious of all were those of Chism.

Chism . . .

She blinked suddenly, and pulled herself from the dreamy state she'd drifted into.

There was something wrong with Chism, she knew, and she had no idea what it was. They'd spoken on the telephone every night, but the conversations had become shorter and shorter. He hadn't said anything that distressed her, but she'd sensed a strange undercurrent in him and could no longer deny that things just weren't right.

She grabbed her keys and purse and hurried to the front door. As she entered the house, she instantly realized no one was there.

Without going a step farther, she was acutely aware of the house's emptiness. A stillness, a strange hollowness, enveloped it. The house seemed to be crying out that no one lived there.

She walked forward cautiously, her gaze sweeping over the living room. The ashes in the fireplace were a dead, dull gray, and no wood was stacked next to the hearth. No newspapers, magazines, or books lay scattered on the end tables, showing how Chism had spent his evenings.

A chill swept over Minta as she rushed on to the kitchen. Her breath caught as she flung open the refrigerator door and stared at the empty shelves.

Dear Lord, where was Chism? This was crazy. She'd called him every might, there at Willow Hill, at exactly seven o'clock. But there was no evidence, not even a glass in the sink, to indicate that he had ever been there.

She ran through the house and up the stairs, a sob escaping from her lips as she again found no sign of anything that belonged to Chism. As she stood in the middle of her bedroom, she told herself to calm down. Chism hadn't known she was returning to Haven Port that day. She'd got a call from the manager of the radio station late last night, saying they were accepting her advertising package. Early that morning, she'd got up to start the long drive to Maine, wanting to surprise Chism.

But his not knowing about her arrival would only explain why Chism wasn't there at the moment. From everything she'd seen, he wasn't staying at Willow Hill at all. But she'd spoken to him every night at seven o'clock!

She pressed her fingertips to her throbbing temples, trying to think clearly.

Where was Chism?

What on earth was going on here?

She narrowed her eyes, pursed her lips, and marched from the room.

Arminta Masterson Westerly, she decided, was going to find out. Chism Talbert had disappeared all those years ago, shattering her heart, and she'd be damned if he was going to do it again.

"Not on your life, buster," she muttered grimly as she slid into her car.

She sped down the road with great determination, but by the time she parked by Chism's house, her heart was racing and her knees trembling. His father's old truck was in the narrow driveway, indicating he was there. With more bravado than she actually possessed, she knocked firmly on the front door of the small house.

A few moments later the door was opened, and Chism stared at her in surprise.

Do not fling yourself into this man's arms and kiss him senseless, Minta told herself. But he was so handsome, and she loved him so much . . .

"Chism," she said coolly, lifting her chin. "Fancy meeting you here. I expected, silly me, to find you at home."

His eyebrows drew together in a frown. "I *am* home."

"I see. May I come in?"

He stepped back to allow her to enter. As he closed the door, she turned to face him.

"It's quite obvious, Chism," she said, wishing her voice were a bit stronger, "that you haven't been living at Willow Hill since I left."

"No, I haven't," he said quietly.

"Yet you were there every night when I called. Would you care to explain what kind of game you're playing?"

"I'm not playing any game, Minta. I'm facing facts. I went to Willow Hill long enough to receive your call, then came back here to where I belong. I felt this discussion was better held in person, rather than on the phone. If I had know you were returning today, I would have been at Willow Hill."

"To say what?"

"That this isn't going to work. You and I, together. Dammit, Minta, I love you, but I can't pretend any longer that we exist in the same world."

"I don't understand," she said, sinking onto the edge of a chair.

"My father was right," he said, sounding defeated. "He told me countless times that I should accept who I was and not attempt to be what I wasn't. He made certain that I stayed in my own world that long-ago summer, and now *I'm* reaching that decision on my own. Yes, I've got a lot of money, all the material possessions I could possibly want, but the fact remains that I'm from this side of the inlet. I'm a Mainer, and you're one of the summer people."

"Chism—"

"No," he said, raising one hand to silence her. "I belong here in this house, Minta, but you don't. I don't belong at Willow Hill, but you do. Different worlds. I've been taking second place in your life this past week. Your world called to you, and you went. I can't live that way. It's over between us. It has to be, because there's no other way open to us."

Minta searched frantically within herself for an emotion to cling to other than heartache and despair. She found and held fast . . . to anger.

She stood up, forced one foot in front of the other, and crossed the room to stand toe-to-toe with Chism. She tipped her head back to meet his gaze, and glowered at him.

"You listen to me, Chism Talbert," she said fiercely. "The fact that I agreed to marry you does *not* mean that I take on the roles of wife and mother and forget about me, the woman, the person. Yes, I went after that radio-station job, and I got it. It was important to me, *but* not the most important thing in my life. I compromised, Chism. I put in sixteen-hour days to accomplish what I needed to do, so that I could come home to you as quickly as possible."

"Minta—"

"Shut up. Chism Talbert, you are a snob. I come from the wrong side of the inlet, so I don't measure up to your standards. Well, tough toasties, you creep, because I love you, and I'm going to compromise, meet you half-way on every issue, until I wear you down and you marry me. Your father was wrong, Chism. We're blending our worlds, taking the best from both, to create one that is just for us."

"I—"

"I refuse to have my heart broken again. Do you hear me, Talbert? This class-distinction stuff of yours stinks, and I've had enough of it. I belong here, dammit, and I belong in New

York too. So do you, Chism. And we'll belong in the world we make for ourselves and for our children. I belong, belong, belong, and you're not going to take that away from me. I love you. But I swear to heaven, if you don't stop acting like an idiot, I'm going to deck you!"

Chism stared at her for a long moment before he spoke.

"Are you finished?" he asked.

She sniffed indignantly. "Yes."

"You're in love with a snob who is a creep and an idiot? That doesn't say much for your taste in men."

"I never claimed to be perfect. Loving you may not be the brightest thing I've ever done, but that's the way it is."

He smiled slowly. "You're a holy terror once you get going, Minta Westerly."

"Don't push me, Chism Talbert."

His smile faded. "I won't push you. I plan to love you for the rest of my life. Everything you just said . . . well, yelled . . . was true. I was scared to death, Minta, so I took the safe road, the one my father insisted I should stay on. But he was wrong, I was wrong, and I'm sorry. We *do* belong, wherever we choose to be. We'll be husband and wife, and father and mother, but we'll be man and woman, individual people, as well. Minta, forgive me, please."

"Oh, Chism," she sighed. "Of course I forgive you."

He framed her face in his hands. "Arminta

Masterson Westerly, will you marry me? Will you be my wife, my partner, my love, my life, for all time?"

"Oh, yes, Chism, yes, and we'll cherish every memory we make . . . together."

"I think I'd better confess something."

"What is it?"

"While you were gone, I painted your bike yellow."

She laughed and flung her arms around his neck. "I'll adore it, and so will the next Arminta, the one who will be evidence of our love."

Then shiny yellow bicycles were forgotten, as Arminta Masterson Westerly and Chism Talbert created exquisitely beautiful memories.

Willow Hill
Christmas Eve, 1893

Dear Diary,

 How wonderful to be visiting Willow Hill and to be sitting in my favorite bay window once again.

 We came from the city two days ago and met Mama and Papa here for an old-fashioned white Christmas. Joseph and Papa went out earlier today and cut a magnificent tree, which we all decorated as we sang Christmas carols.

 How happy Joseph and I are. His landscaping business is growing larger, and he is constantly hiring more workers. We just purchased a lovely ancient house that we are going to renovate ourselves, together.

 I must dash, dear diary, as it is feeding

time for a very precious little baby. She is Joseph's and my daughter, Arminta Masterson Westerly. We have started what we hope will become a family tradition of naming the first girl Arminta. My imagination dances forward in time to all the Armintas yet to come.

Merry Christmas, dear diary. I await the new year eagerly, anticipating each day, each night, and all the glorious memories.

Good night.

Sincerely,

Arminta Masterson Westerly

THE EDITOR'S CORNER

And what is so rare as a day in June?
Then, if ever, come perfect days . . .

With apologies to James Russell Lowell I believe we can add *and perfect reading, too, from LOVESWEPT and FANFARE . . .*

As fresh and beautiful as the rose in its title SAN ANTONIO ROSE, LOVESWEPT #474, by Fran Baker is a thrilling way to start your romance reading next month. Rafe Martinez betrayed Jeannie Crane, but her desire still burned for the only man she'd ever loved, the only man who'd ever made love to her. Rafe was back and admitting to her that her own father had driven him away. When he learned her secret, Rafe had a sure-fire way to get revenge . . . but would he? And could Jeannie ever find a way to tame the maverick who still drove her wild with ecstasy? This unforgettable love story will leave you breathless. . . .

Perfect in its powerful emotion is TOUGH GUY, SAVVY LADY, LOVESWEPT #475, by Charlotte Hughes. Charlotte tells a marvelous story of overwhelming love and stunning self-discovery in this tale of beautiful Honey Buchannan and Lucas McKay. Lucas smothered her with his love, sweetly dominating her life—and when she leaves he is distraught, but determined to win her back. Lucas has always hidden his own fears—he's a man who has pulled himself up by his boot straps to gain fortune and position—but to recapture the woman who is his life, he is going to have to change. TOUGH GUY, SAVVY LADY will touch you deeply . . . and joyfully.

Little could be so rare as being trapped IN A GOLDEN WEB, Courtney Henke's LOVESWEPT #476. Heroine Elizabeth Hammer is desperate! Framed for a crime she didn't commit, she's driven to actions she never dreamed she was capable of taking. And kidnapping gorgeous hunk Dexter Wolffe and forcing him to take her to Phoenix is just the start. Dex plays along—finding the beautiful bank manager the most delectable adversary he's ever encountered. He wants to kiss her defiant mouth and make her his prisoner . . . of love. You'll thrill to the romance of these two loners on the lam in one of LOVESWEPT's most delightful offerings ever!

And a dozen American beauties to Glenna McReynolds for her fabulously inventive OUTLAW CARSON, LOVESWEPT #478. We'll wager you've never run into a hero like Kit Carson before. Heroine Kristine Richards certainly hasn't. When the elusive, legendary Kit shows up at her university, Kristine can only wonder if he's a smuggler, a scholar—or a blessing from heaven, sent to shatter her senses. Kit is shocked by Kristine . . . for he had never believed before meeting her that there was any woman on earth who could arouse in him such fierce hunger . . . or such desperate jealousy. Both are burdened with secrets and wary of each other and have a long and difficult labyrinth to struggle through. But there are glimpses ahead of a Shangri-la just for them! As dramatic and surprising as a budding rose in winter, OUTLAW CARSON will enchant you!

Welcome to Tonya Wood who makes her debut with us with a real charmer in LOVESWEPT #477, GORGEOUS. Sam Christie was just too good-looking to be real. And too talented. And women were always throwing themselves at him. Well, until Mercy Rose Sullivan appeared in his life. When Mercy rescues Sam from the elevator in their apartment building, he can't believe what an endearing gypsy she is—or that she doesn't recognize him! Mercy is as feisty as she is guileless and puts up a terrific fight against Sam's long, slow, deep kisses. His fame is driving them apart just as love is bursting into full bloom . . . and it seems that only a miracle can bring these two dreamers together, where they belong. Sheer magical romance!

What is more perfect to read about on a perfect day than a long, lean, mean deputy sheriff and a lady locksmith who's been called to free him from the bed he is handcuffed to? Nothing! So run to pick-up your copy of SILVER BRACELETS, LOVE-SWEPT #479, by Sandra Chastain. You'll laugh and cry and root for these two unlikely lovers to get together. Sarah Wilson is as tenderhearted as they come. Asa Canyon is one rough, tough hombre who has always been determined to stay free of emotional entanglements. They taste ecstasy together . . . but is Sarah brave enough to risk loving such a man? And can Asa dare to believe that a woman will always be there for him? A romance as vivid and fresh and thrilling as a crimson rose!

And don't forget FANFARE next month with its irresistible longer fiction.

First, STORM WINDS by Iris Johansen. This thrilling, sweeping novel set against the turbulent times of the French Revolution continues with stories of those whose lives are touched by the fabled Wind Dancer. Two unforgettable pairs of lovers will have you singing the praises of Iris Johansen all summer long! DREAMS TO KEEP by Nomi Berger is a powerfully moving novel of a memorable and courageous woman, a survivor of the Warsaw ghetto, who defies all odds and builds a life and a fortune in America. But she is a woman who will risk everything for revenge on the man who condemned her family . . . until a love that is larger than life itself gives her a vision of a future of which she'd never dreamed. And all you LOVESWEPT readers will know you have to be sure to get a copy of MAGIC by Tami Hoag in which the fourth of the "fearsome foursome" gets a love for all time. This utterly enchanting love story shows off the best of Tami Hoag! Remember, FANFARE signals that something great is coming. . . .

Enjoy your perfect days to come with perfect reading from LOVESWEPT and FANFARE!

With every good wish,

Carolyn Nichols

Carolyn Nichols
Editor
LOVESWEPT
Bantam Books
666 Fifth Avenue
New York, NY 10103

She was as brave as she was beautiful, but could she win the heart of a gunfighter who swore he'd never settle down?

THE BONNIE BLUE
by Joan Elliott Pickart

Slade Ironbow was big, dark, and dangerous, a man any woman would want -- and the one rancher Becca Colton found impossible to resist!

Nobody could tame the rugged half-Apache with the devil's eyes, but when honor and a secret promise brought him to the Bonnie Blue ranch as her new foreman, Becca couldn't send him away. She needed his help to keep from losing her ranch to the man she suspected had murdered her father, but stubborn pride made her fight the mysterious loner whose body left her breathless and whose touch made her burn with needs she'd never understood. Slade was drawn to Becca's fire and fury, but hated losing control in the seductive duel their hearts waged.

Could Becca help him find a home in her arms, once her mother's legacy of love was finally theirs to cherish?

The Bonnie Blue. Available in June wherever Bantam Fanfare Books are sold.

THE LATEST IN BOOKS AND AUDIO CASSETTES

Paperbacks

☐	28671	**NOBODY'S FAULT** Nancy Holmes	$5.95
☐	28412	**A SEASON OF SWANS** Celeste De Blasis	$5.95
☐	28354	**SEDUCTION** Amanda Quick	$4.50
☐	28594	**SURRENDER** Amanda Quick	$4.50
☐	28435	**WORLD OF DIFFERENCE** Leonia Blair	$5.95
☐	28416	**RIGHTFULLY MINE** Doris Mortman	$5.95
☐	27032	**FIRST BORN** Doris Mortman	$4.95
☐	27283	**BRAZEN VIRTUE** Nora Roberts	$4.50
☐	27891	**PEOPLE LIKE US** Dominick Dunne	$4.95
☐	27260	**WILD SWAN** Celeste De Blasis	$5.95
☐	25692	**SWAN'S CHANCE** Celeste De Blasis	$5.95
☐	27790	**A WOMAN OF SUBSTANCE** Barbara Taylor Bradford	$5.95

Audio

☐ **SEPTEMBER** by Rosamunde Pilcher
Performance by Lynn Redgrave
180 Mins. Double Cassette   45241-X $15.95

☐ **THE SHELL SEEKERS** by Rosamunde Pilcher
Performance by Lynn Redgrave
180 Mins. Double Cassette   48183-9 $14.95

☐ **COLD SASSY TREE** by Olive Ann Burns
Performance by Richard Thomas
180 Mins. Double Cassette   45166-9 $14.95

☐ **NOBODY'S FAULT** by Nancy Holmes
Performance by Geraldine James
180 Mins. Double Cassette   45250-9 $14.95

Bantam Books, Dept. FBS, 414 East Golf Road, Des Plaines, IL 60016

Please send me the items I have checked above. I am enclosing $_____
(please add $2.50 to cover postage and handling). Send check or money order,
no cash or C.O.D.s please. (Tape offer good in USA only.)

Mr/Ms _____

Address _____

City/State _____ Zip _____

Please allow four to six weeks for delivery.   FBS–1/91
Prices and availability subject to change without notice.

60 Minutes to a Better, More Beautiful You!

Now it's easier than ever to awaken your sensuality, stay slim forever—even make yourself irresistible. With Bantam's bestselling subliminal audio tapes, you're only 60 minutes away from a better, more beautiful you!

__ 45004-2	**Slim Forever**	$8.95
__ 45035-2	**Stop Smoking Forever**	$8.95
__ 45022-0	**Positively Change Your Life**	$8.95
__ 45041-7	**Stress Free Forever**	$8.95
__ 45106-5	**Get a Good Night's Sleep**	$7.95
__ 45094-8	**Improve Your Concentration**	$7.95
__ 45172-3	**Develop A Perfect Memory**	$8.95

Bantam Books, Dept. LT, 414 East Golf Road, Des Plaines, IL 60016

Please send me the items I have checked above. I am enclosing $_____ (please add $2.50 to cover postage and handling). Send check or money order, no cash or C.O.D.s please. (Tape offer good in USA only.)

Mr/Ms _____

Address _____

City/State _____ Zip _____

LT-2/91

Please allow four to six weeks for delivery.
Prices and availability subject to change without notice.

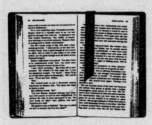